Gift of Desperation

A Claire Sebastian Novel

Robin M. Gilliam
Web of Life Art Studio

Photograph of author by Dirk Gilliam
Artwork used on cover by Robin M. Gilliam
Cover design by Liz G. Merchant

ACKNOWLEDGEMENTS

I am grateful for the continued love and support of my husband, Dirk Gilliam; my parents, Jay Fred and Sunny Cohen; my sister, Lisa Caplan and her family. I very much appreciate: Loris Nebbia, author of *Solomon's Puzzle,* for mentoring me and providing content editing; Liz G. Merchant for the beautiful cover; Carlie Caplan as my copy editor; my test readers: Joanna, Anne, and Sunny; and last but not least, everyone who has supported me on this journey.

This book is dedicated to Dirk

There is a danger in not expressing your feelings.

There is an even greater danger in not knowing what your feelings are.

Goucher College 1984-1986 Catalog

Chapter One

As her eyes adjusted to the light sneaking in from the drawn blinds, Claire Sebastian realized she was in a strange room tangled in the arms of a naked, snoring man. She tried to sneak out of bed, but caught a whiff of his noxious breath—a mixture of stale beer and sex—and tumbled to the floor instead, taking the sheet with her. The man grumbled grabbing the pillow, let out a loud fart, and snuggled back into dream land.

As Claire found her footing, she threw the sheet on him. She then followed, "I Can't Get No Satisfaction," by the Rolling Stones to her purse where she found her buried cell phone. It was her best friend, Lexie, one of the "Four Amigos" from her college days.

"How was it? He was gorgeous!" Lexie screeched.

"Great," Claire whispered; wishing she could remember. "But I can't really talk now."

"Oh, okay!" Lexie said, "I'll call you later."

Claire thought she might be sick as she searched for her *screw me now* outfit. First she scrambled into her peach silk bra and panties. Then she pulled on her tight aqua V neck t-shirt that revealed her ample cleavage. It made her shoulder-length, straight brown hair shine like honey, and turned her hazel eyes into the color of the Caribbean Sea.

The night started to crystallize in her mind as Claire shimmied into her skinny brown jeans that made her small butt pop just enough to say, *like the junk in my trunk?* The bridal shower—at the bar—the guy. He was gorgeous and he was talking to her! The anxiety about the bridal shower and being the last woman standing in the marriage arena was replaced by excitement for the attention, and the prospect of love. The drinks were strong, the music was loud, and he wanted her. Her!

What was his name? Michael, Mike, Mitch. Did they use a condom? *Jesus, what if she got pregnant, aids, or another sexually-transmitted disease?* Before she skulked out of the apartment, she stopped to look through his mail where she found it; his name was Mitch. She took a picture with her phone and wrote a note with her name and number in case he wanted to reach her. She slid on her cowboy boots and left.

The bright sun temporarily blinded Claire. Looking for a taxi she began to search frantically in her purse. *Where was it?* She knew she put it in there before going out last night. The harder she looked, the more anxious she got, finding it difficult to breath. Her hand grabbed her wallet—*No!* Her Keys—*No!* Her Cellphone—*No! No! No!* As her hand felt the shiny cold metal, she breathed a sigh of relief and said out loud, "There you are!" The vodka she kept for emergencies.

What was the emergency? Oh yea, her head hurt, her eyes stung, and her coochy-coochy was sore. *Wow, what kind of sex did we have?* It was probably great sex if her privates hurt that much.

She took a good long pull from her flask, and within seconds she felt the warmth steal down her throat and across her chest—*ahhhh*—*much better*. It filled her up; energized her. *Forget the taxi*, she decided instead to walk to the metro and do her Sunday shopping.

At home, Tabitha, her cat was waiting for her. Claire unpacked her groceries, took a long, hot shower and relaxed for the rest of the day. She continued to nurse her hangover with vodka but was careful to drink only enough to take the edge off; she didn't want to have a hangover for work tomorrow.

Chapter Two

On Monday morning, Claire dressed in fresh black slacks and a clean, crisp, peach blouse buttoned almost to the top. Sporting her tennis shoes and sunglasses she walked the couple blocks to her job at the National Museum of Women in the Arts, known by most D.C. locals as the "NMWA."

On the way, she enjoyed the architecture of the city buildings and breathed in the fresh, morning air, hoping to release the slight pounding in her temples. She stopped for a breakfast sandwich and ordered a cup of coffee with two shots of espresso to ensure she got enough caffeine to carry her to lunch.

She barely made it through the ornate building—once a grand theatre—when her boss, a medium height, heavy-set, Jamaican woman with imposing brown eyes, accosted her.

"Good morning Claire." June said, "The board has decided that you will curate the next show."

Claire's eyes lit up. She had been a junior curator at the NMWA for the past four years, following someone else around, always following their lead. She wanted to be in charge of her own show. Actually, at 28, Claire really just wanted to be in charge.

"The show's title is *Art and Healing,*" June told her.

Claire was taken aback, almost felt like someone had slapped her hard across the face. Claire would not be depicting an artistic movement, such as the Renaissance and how each artist's pieces fit into and supported that movement. *No!* She was going to curate a show around a theme about *Art and Healing.*

Claire's background was art history—clear, distinct lines around what art was and where it fits into history—a neat, little box from where to view her world. *What does Art and Healing mean anyway?*

"*Art and Healing?*" she asked June, hoping that her voice was not so much whiney as inquisitive, looking for more direction.

"Yes!" June said, looking like a giant, gum bubble ready to burst. "We just received an eclectic collection spanning a woman's life, including diaries. We started to read the diaries and were enthralled by her creative expression and using art as a tool to help her heal through life's journey. We want to give you this opportunity to take the lead on this show to provide our visitors with a new way to approach art."

Claire's head was splitting, not just from Saturday night's hangover, but the direction of this assignment.

"Who is the artist?" Claire asked.

"Anonymous," June exclaimed, "The collection was donated along with a very generous grant."

So that explains it, it's always about the money. Never about what I really need!

Through gritted teeth and a smile Claire said, "I appreciate the opportunity and will get started right away."

With that, Claire headed to her office.

Chapter Three

C laire tried to finish her breakfast and cold coffee before changing into her low pumps which lived in her bottom desk drawer. Taking a deep breath, she grabbed her laptop and reluctantly headed to the special exhibits gallery to start working on the *Art and Healing* show. The gallery was already boarded up to the public with an "under construction" notice forcing her to enter through the staff entrance.

Cardboard boxes of all sizes were stacked against the back wall making the gallery smell like an old stuffy attic. She had no idea what to expect and decided to just dive in. She would review and catalog each piece for its place in the show, its description for the program, and the "See for Yourself" cards that the NMWA provided as a courtesy to patrons.

She took out the first brown paper package and unwrapped it hastily jabbing her finger on something sharp.

What the fuck? Why is there something sharp on a piece of artwork? What have I gotten myself into? The pounding in her head got louder.

She slowed down now, taking her time to unwrap the artwork to avoid injuring herself. It wasn't one piece; it was three abstract collages. She turned the first piece over and noticed the title, "Shattered." *Shattered?* She looked closer at the piece. It was very heavy, both physically and emotionally.

The first collage was created on a wood foundation covered in a striking black, red, and grey silk fabric. The artist used additional strips of the same fabric to create sculptured hills and valleys in which to house found objects. These included thick, sharp, broken mirror pieces, watch parts and faces, and a fake pearl necklace tying everything together—very bold and a little unnerving.

Claire's heart stopped for a minute. *Am I shattered? What did the artist mean? What was she trying to work through? Is this where the artist's healing started?* Claire remembered the artist's diaries and rushed to find them. *The date, what was the date of the artwork?* She searched until she found the reflection on "Shattered."

Dear Diary...I couldn't wait to tear up that dress. It stood for hope, but look at the mess I got myself into. How did it happen? A marriage, the beginning of a life together, turned dark and evil. Was it my fault? How could he? Was it the drugs running through the relationship? I am so stupid to trust, to expect hope. Was I wrong to expect a marriage of respect, compassion, passion? Passion turned to rage. How could he—Rage turned against me...

The entry stopped and Claire caught her breath. *Was I, I mean the artist—raped? What happened?* She took a step back and really looked at this piece. She caught a glimpse of herself in the three large mirror shards set against fabric the color of fresh blood. She felt sweaty and uncomfortable; her clothes felt too tight. She wanted to escape.

—She was eight, snuggled in her bed and he was letting in the cold air as he moved the blanket off her, but not to hug her goodnight, no, to touch her. His hand moved under her favorite cotton nightshirt with Disney's Arial swimming freely in the sea. As his one hand continued to move down, down, the other hand was clamped over her mouth telling her it was their little secret—

Laughter from the hall brought Claire back to the gallery where tears sprung to her eyes; she closed them tightly and tried to gain control. She looked at her watch, 3pm, two hours until work was over and she could get a drink to forget.

Or rather, to stop the memories of the day when she tore up her nightgown.

***

How she couldn't stop until she had shredded that thing. How her father found the mess and beat her for it. How she ran fast to Aunt Jo's. How Aunt Jo calmly stopped binding the quilt, put down the needle and thread, and soothed her wounds with her magic medicine and touch. How she asked Aunt Jo if she could please come and live with her.

"Evi lives with you," Claire remembers begging, "Why can't I? Don't you love me like you love Evi?"

"Sure do love you lots and lots, and wish you could, but he won't allow it," said Aunt Jo.

Claire knew who "he" was—her father and Aunt Jo's brother.

"But I am always here; right next door. So run fast to me when trouble starts."

***

Claire let the memory slip away and was wiping away her tears as a tall middle-aged black man wearing a standard blue NWMA, staff uniform walked in.

"How is Claire today," Herb asked as he handed her a tissue.

"Ok Herb. Just started working on this weird collection. And between you and me, I have no idea how anyone can call this art. I really just want to go hang out with the portraits in the 17th century gallery and marvel at how those women artists created such lifelike portraits, jewelry and all. Not worrying if I am going to slice my finger open on a raw edge of broken mirror. Really! How is this art?" Claire almost cried.

"I don't know my little bear," an enduring term Herb often used with Claire, "But if you keep your heart open you might just get that message you are looking for. Let me know when you are ready for me to help you hang the pieces. Just buzz me and keep that beautiful smile lit up."

"Will do," Claire said as Herb slipped out the door.

***

The second piece that Claire pulled from the package was entitled, "Go Forth, Lady Bug." It was built on a wood foundation and painted black before the same silk fabric used in "Shattered" was added as a large oval. Again, the artist created three-dimensional texture and pattern through sculpted pieces of fabric. The hills and valleys are embellished with buttons, jewelry pieces, and chains; no broken mirror pieces. *Thank goodness!* At first glance, this too looked like an abstract collage, but a closer look showed a sad face.

Dear Diary...I made this piece as a continuation of "Shattered." I no longer feel as shattered so didn't include any broken mirror pieces. After I laid the fabric foundation, the shape reminded me of a lady bug and lady bugs are positive symbols for me. I felt I could move forward as a survivor, move away from being a victim...

Reading through the artist's diary, Claire wondered if she was a victim or a survivor. She didn't know and wasn't sure if she really cared. All she did know was that the only way to cope was to fly to safety like the ladybug in the artwork. Taking a drink took her to that safe place—so did being in a man's arms, away from the cruel, hard world, until—*were those things still working*? As fast as the question surfaced, it drowned away at the thought of a nice glass of wine and the strong arms of a man.

***

Claire removed the third collage in this series, entitled "Now What?" It was built on a wood foundation painted a dark, forest green. She used a gold fabric to create an "X" in the center as the foundation for the collage. The artist built hills and valleys with a complimentary pattern of blue, red and gold fabric draped across and around the "X" which were then embellished with similar items as found in the other two pieces. The artist has extraordinary use of color and placement of found objects to keep the viewer's eye moving and interpreting her work.

The viewer is drawn in and invited to engage with the piece, seeing again and again a reference to time—to being stuck in time—the upside down watch faces, and the multiple stickers with days of the week repeated over and over again.

Dear Diary...I started to experiment with different fabrics, moving away from feeling shattered toward becoming whole again. I felt playful mixing rusty, hardware pieces with watch faces, with shiny beads and jewelry pieces and chains. Like the title, "Now What?" states, I am moving forward but to where—I don't know yet...

Claire didn't really see what was so important about this piece in relation to healing. All she knew was that the only thing she wanted to move toward was a drink to stop time and keep the memories at bay.

To finish for the day, she called Herb and together they hung the three collages. She saved the descriptions that she drafted for each piece and locked up the gallery. Herb walked her to her office so they could return her laptop for safekeeping.

On his way out Herb said, "See you tomorrow and be safe, little bear."

"You too, Herb, and thanks for your help."

***

Claire blew out a long breath as she left the NMWA. She was drained from struggling to forget memories that were pushing up like weeds in a garden. She was ready to go home and curl up with a glass of wine and a sexy man. While she wasn't sure where she was going to find a man on a Monday night, she did know where there was wine. She knew she couldn't touch the hard stuff until the weekend, and *wine wasn't really alcohol anyway, was it?*

With that thought, Claire turned off the light, locked her office door and headed home.

Chapter Four

On Tuesday morning, Claire woke up on the sofa in her wrinkled work clothes with a slight headache—*a hangover?* How could she have a hangover, she only drank wine. Looking at the empty bottle on the coffee table, she thought, *how much wine did I drink? Was the bottle full when I got home? Probably not*—but she couldn't be sure. *Oh well, no harm done* Claire thought.

She showered and dressed casually because she was hanging a show and the public would not see her. She popped some Tylenol, noticing that the bottle was almost empty, and made a mental note to get some more on the way home.

She stopped at the McDonalds across the street from the NMWA to grab a quick breakfast and huge coffee drink before heading into work. There was a no food/drink rule in the galleries, but she didn't care, she was working on a show, not a guest viewing one, so she took her breakfast and coffee into the *Art and Healing* gallery. *I really hate this collection*, Claire thought waiting for the Tylenol to ease her throbbing head.

Claire found three abstract collages in the next box she unpacked. These pieces used mirrors as their foundation. *What is up with this three business*, Claire thought, annoyed. *How many pieces of artwork did this artist need to create to heal? What the hell was wrong with her anyway? Bitch*! She was glad she did not say that out loud because exactly at that moment June walked into the gallery.

Claire offered her beautiful smile to assure June that everything was moving along and showed her the progress she had made. Wishing she could say, *hey bitch, I only started yesterday, how much fucking progress do you think I made?*

June was pleased and left, but not before reminding Claire of how to hang the write-up for each piece already hung on the wall. Claire had been at the museum for four years and did not feel she needed to be told how to hang the descriptions.

With a sweet smile still on her face Claire said, "Will do, thanks." What she really wanted to say was, *Fuck off!*

***

Again, Claire's head started to pound. Or maybe it never really stopped. She had finished her breakfast and was reaching for the coffee when she knocked it over causing a tsunami of brown liquid to threaten the opened box of artwork. Slipping and almost falling, Claire quickly moved the box away. She caught her breath and hoped like hell that her pounding heart would quiet down so that no one else would hear it, especially June and come running back.

What is wrong with me, Claire questioned. Trembling, she used the remaining napkins from her breakfast to start cleaning up the mess. She got some much needed paper towels from the nearby cleaning closet to finish soaking up her despair. Herb miraculously appeared with a mop, and together they got rid of the evidence. She finished what was left in the coffee cup, hoping to capture enough caffeine to set her straight for the rest of the morning. But no such luck.

***

The first piece Claire took out was entitled, "Now You See Me, Now You Don't." It was a round mirror, with only one half filled with an abstract collage of the black, red, and grey silk fabric sculpted into mountains and valleys, then embellished with plastic and wood beads.

Dear Diary...I started to collect full, not shattered mirrors, the better to see myself clearly in, and decided to create a collage using half the mirror. I guess I am not ready to see all of me yet. What is wrong with me that nobody seemed to love me for me? What is wrong with me that a boyfriend that I loved cheated on me with an older, frumpier woman—when I was cute and little? What is wrong with me that a husband rapes me? So, the collaged half of the mirror reflects this confusion, while the mirror side lets me see me for me and says, "You are ok." But am I? Not sure which side to focus on...

As Claire looked at this piece, she saw herself clearly in both halves, especially the collaged half. In the mirror section, she did not see a grown woman; instead she saw a small child, helpless and scared, wanting only to be safe. In the collaged side, she saw the grown woman, struggling to find that safety. Shaking away these thoughts, Claire continued to examine the artwork.

***

In the second mirrored piece entitled "Grandma's Luv," the artist continued to indulge her abstract style. She incorporated a mirror in the shape of an upside down heart. She used the mirror as part of the artwork by covering only a third of it with sculpted fabric. She incorporated driftwood as part of the collage and as a functional piece for hanging it. She also embellished this piece with shells, a large green marble and other found objects.

> Dear Diary... The fabric was a piece of my grandmother's clothing. I think it was a scarf that was attached to a beige blouse that reminded me of her. I always felt closest to my grandmother and very loved, so I wanted to recreate that feeling by creating with her stuff. I started to collect more from nature, like the 15 million year old shells, and worked them also into my artwork...

As Claire observed this piece, she felt calm and loved. It reminded her of Aunt Jo and all the times she flew over to her house to escape to safety. Even though they stayed in touch through email and FaceTime, Claire really missed her Aunt Jo. This piece also made Claire a little sad as she realized that she did not miss her own mother, *at all.*

How could Aunt Jo be so different from her mother? Aunt Jo was warm and loving, strong and confident. Claire's mom was cold and unavailable, meek like a mouse, and always cowering. Claire wasn't sure how her mom and Aunt Jo were best friends. Claire didn't want to go back there right now, so she tried to focus on the next piece.

***

For the last piece in this series, the artist used a 1920s, antique blue, stop-sign-shaped mirror. She built an abstract collage around it using sculpted, stiffened fabric, driftwood for supports, and on it she hung rusty pieces and shells, glass and jewelry parts. Again, the viewer could only experience herself in part of the mirror.

Dear Diary...I went antiquing this weekend and found this blue antique mirror—which I absolutely love! I also love the fabric I chose for the collage for its metallic colors and how it responded to Stiffy. I had discovered how to stiffen fabric into flowing mountains and valleys like I had learned to shape clay. The peaks and valleys I sculpted continue to reflect my journey in finding me. I left about a quarter of this mirror exposed since I am still not ready to accept me. I had a hard time with this piece, trying to attach the driftwood and chains to make it hang correctly on the wall. It still does not hang straight on the wall—but neither do I—sometimes I really hate myself despite the way I look to the outside world. Like the beauty in this piece of artwork, I appear put-together, but like the driftwood holding it up on the wall, I too can fall apart at any moment...

Claire found this piece intriguing. The blue of the mirror was mystical, while the driftwood designed to frame and hold the piece seemed fragile, similar to how she felt. She couldn't believe that the artist had said that she hated herself—sometimes. She was starting to connect with the artist, which she didn't like. *I like myself, don't I?* It wasn't really like she would fall apart at any minute, if the glue holding her together dissolved. Would she—fall apart, that is?

Herb showed up and hung the three pieces, while Claire printed out the six descriptions from the last two days. She hung them exactly as June told her to even though she already knew how. *Micromanaging bitch*, she fumed; glad she didn't say that out loud also. If she were texting or tweeting this, she would add LOL since she suddenly wanted to laugh hysterically.

***

On the way home, Claire's head was about to explode, reminding her to stop and get a big bottle of Tylenol and Advil (just in case the Tylenol didn't work.) She also stopped to replenish her bar with a few more bottles of wine and a six-pack of beer. Claire wanted to make sure she was stocked up for when friends stopped by.

Chapter Five

On Wednesday morning, as Claire made her way through the next carton in the *Art and Healing* collection, she felt a hard, box like structure. *What the hell is this*? She took it out carefully, even though she wanted to yank it out, damaging it, so she wouldn't have to deal with it.

What she wouldn't give to be safe and secure rotating recognizable portraits in the permanent Renaissance collection. However, when she unwrapped this piece, she recognized the "canvas;" it was a drawer from an antique wood sewing table. How she loved those tables. The drawer's ornate handle took Claire back eighteen years to when she was ten and visited Aunt Jo.

—Aunt Jo's was a safe haven that was nowhere to be found in her house. Claire's house was just a structure to live in. Aunt Jo's house was a home. Whenever Claire went over there, Aunt Jo was sewing a traditional quilt. Her quilts were all over the house. Claire had a favorite, well used, double wedding ring quilt that she loved to curl up in and watch Aunt Jo create. The whirl of the machine, Aunt Jo going in and out of those wood drawers took Claire to a quiet, safe place, away from the shouting and rage that lived next door—

As she held "The Drawer," it reminded her of "Shattered," because of the same thick, broken mirror pieces glued to its bottom. The artist had drilled holes on the sides of the drawer and wove metal wire back and forth, stringing red, black, silver, and maroon beads within the drawer, suspended above the broken mirror pieces and on the outside of the box. The artist attached a metal hanger to the bottom of the drawer so it would hang straight on the wall.

Dear Diary...In creating the woven boxes, I felt a need to stitch me up. I still felt very broken and shattered like the thick jagged mirror pieces I glued to the box bottoms. Creating these boxes is a way for me to continue moving from victim to survivor. One day I feel strong, like I can climb Mount Everest, and the next day I am falling, spiraling down into a deep dark crevasse. I don't like the darkness and need to find the light and the only thing that works for me is to create. I love using found objects. I use watch pieces a lot for they remind me of time wasted, a lost piece of my life, myself—I also use beads of all shapes, colors and sizes for they add color and texture, including a bright shine to add a glimmer of hope. As in my other series, I created three. It seems that by the time I finish the third one, I have climbed out of the hole and found some light and hope—healing a little bit...

After reading the artist's diary, Claire fished through the collection and found the other two pieces. She could almost feel the hope the artist was striving for, but not quite. The thick mirror shards still reflected back a broken, shattered, little girl living in a woman's body.

God, how she hated this collection and the memories it dragged up. But Claire was starting to understand why the artist created in a series of three. By the time Claire curated the third piece, she too began to feel a little peace herself—just a little bit. *Maybe it did take a lot of creating to get through a painful experience from long, long ago.*

Before Herb joined her to hang "the drawers," fear rushed around and through Claire as she tried to shake off the memories.

***

Claire was glad that she had stocked her bar for company. She was also glad that she was the only one she was expecting.

Chapter Six

On Thursday morning, Claire continued slogging her way through the collection. She felt like she was thigh high in thick mud trying to run in high heels. She removed three heavy pieces wrapped together. *For God's sake,* Claire thought, *another three piece series?* It was torture for Claire to curate just one piece at a time for this show, but a series of three over and over again were driving her crazy. *What is wrong with this artist anyway?*

Back to business she thought. Focusing the best she could, Claire laid each piece on the floor. Each collage was created on a quarter inch wood base covered with a blue satin material and nestled in a gold frame. Each piece included an antique glove holding a tool and was adorned with additional found objects that complimented each other. Again, the artist took the viewer on a journey around the piece with the expert placement of the additional items.

Dear Diary...Losing my grandma was devastating. She was the only one who loved me for who I was. She never judged or criticized me like my other relatives. When I helped to clean out her apartment I found many treasures, including her old gloves and my grandpa's old tools. Something called me to put them together to represent these powerful positive feelings. As I built these collages, my heart started to heal from my loss. I felt my grandparents were still with me, memorialized in these collages...

—Claire was back in Aunt Jo's sewing room curled up under her favorite quilt, reading a book. She had barely escaped another brutal attack by her father. His tools included his fists, cruel, hateful words, and tree branches from the back yard which took apart things, took apart her; disabling and dismantling her—

As Claire came back to the present, and looked at the three pieces of artwork before her, she realized that not all tools are bad. While Aunt Jo used a seam ripper it was not to destroy her quilts, like her father's fists destroyed her. It was to take out the bad stitches. Aunt Jo could then use her sewing machine to sew the quilt right. Maybe Claire was like a quilt, slowly removing the old crooked stitching to be resewn back together.

Claire's head spun as she looked at her arms expecting to see bruises there. She needed a drink to quiet the physical and verbal bruises still unhealed from her youth. With a shudder Claire felt the sweat begin to drip down her back. *I can't take a drink, not now, not during the week, not when I'm working. I can't afford to have a hangover tomorrow; I need to be on top of my game for work.* I think I'll head to the gym instead!

That night after work, Claire hit the gym with a vengeance and took the advanced cycling class for a mind-numbing workout. She also got lucky in that her favorite trainer, Jose, was there— skin the color of a latte—muscles sculpted as Michelangelo's *David*.

She loved her private sessions with him in the gym. One look from her and they met in the back room where old, outdated equipment was stored. Like many times before, without a word, he mounted her on the old cracked weight bench for a fast and furious ride, pumping muscles no other class could touch. Hot, sweaty, and satiated, she was ready to go home. The runner's high she experienced from both workouts numbed her to the point of oblivion.

***

As Claire walked into her apartment, her cell phone rang. She looked at the display and her heart lit up. It was her fiancé, Jeremy. Three years ago they met at her friend, Chastity's wedding; six months ago they got engaged. His six foot frame carried a sturdy, athletic body. He had a nice head of sandy brown hair that framed his white chiseled face. His green eyes were warm and inviting, softening his sharp features. He was an emergency room doctor who was often not available; exactly how Claire liked it.

"Hey," he said warmly, "I was on my way over for dinner but just got called back to the hospital to handle an overflow in the ER."

Still feeling satisfied from the sultry sex with Jose and the need to take a shower, Claire said, "Ohhh, ok, I'll miss you; rain check for tomorrow?"

Tomorrow was Friday and while Claire looked forward to the hunt, a night with Jeremy would be ideal too.

Their love making was more comfortable now, a repeating pattern, the intense hunger replaced by mutual love. But she did love him and being with him filled her up too.

"No, can't this weekend, I am on duty. How about next Tuesday?"

At first a little steamed, and then excited about the opportunity to hunt, she said, "Sure, can't wait. Luv ya."

They hung up. She played with her cat, Tabitha, fed them both, and took that much needed shower. Then she fished in her purse for her engagement ring which she put back on.

Chapter Seven

It was finally Friday and Claire could feel the excitement build as she planned her hunt for that night. She hoped it was *raining men*, like the song said—a stable of hot, horny, straight men to help her forget; she felt like lava waiting to explode from a volcano.

As she walked to work, she passed the new bar she would venture into and her mind accelerated to being bent over one of the pool tables, skirt hiked up around her hips, taking it hard from behind. Coming back to reality, she entered the NMWA almost tripping up the marble stairs. Looking around, she was glad that no one had seen this.

***

Getting settled in the gallery, Claire retrieved the next piece of artwork left out on the floor last night. As she unwrapped it, she felt like someone hit her in the stomach—hard—knocking the wind out of her. It was entitled, "His Things," and sounded like keys rattling together. *What type of artwork makes noise?*

Dear Diary...When I cleaned out my grandma's apartment, I found my grandpa's keys still in their brown leather case and a heart shaped box with "love" engraved on the top. In this collage, I tucked the heart box top into the bowl shaped canvas I made out of a stiffened shirt of grandma's and attached the keys to hang over the opening of the "bowl" to symbolize the unconditional love and acceptance I felt from them...

The sound of the keys in the leather case that looked exactly like her dad's, made Claire catch her breath. How could the artist put a heart with the keys? This absolutely does not symbolize love to her. In fact, it ignited a terror in her like a bomb threat in a subway station.

—*Her mother, Bessie-May, was always "asleep" in her room and, as usual, not available to protect Claire when her father, Ray, got home. Claire's heart would race and her palms would sweat when she heard the sound of her father outside the front door. The sound of keys searching for the lock, dropping,* scratching the door, and dropping again until metal turned metal.

Ray worked physically hard during the week as a stevedore unloading cargo from ships in the Baltimore harbor. During the week he was a functional drunk, only drinking beer. But when he got off on Fridays, Ray and his work buddies hit the hard stuff at the local bars in Fells Point.

While Ray was always a bully during the week, on weekends, he was a mean drunk, whose fists flew into flesh and household goods. Nothing was worth getting attached to in Claire's house because a raging Ray would smash it to bits of nothing in no time flat. They should have bought stock in Sony for as many TVs as they had to replace over the years.

The beatings happened whenever he wanted Claire's help, which seemed like all the time. But no matter what or how Claire did, according to him, she could never do it right. So the yelling started and his fists would fly. Claire was pretty fast, so most of the time she avoided him, running to the arms of Aunt Jo. But even if she avoided the physical assaults, the verbal insults and venom followed her over the fence and through Aunt Jo's door.

Aunt Jo's door was always unlocked for just these occasions. Ray never followed Claire because he could hardly *walk, and Aunt Jo kept a shotgun by her door, which she had threatened her brother with on more than one occasion—*

Shaking, Claire came back to the present. She quickly and professionally wrote up "His Things," and waited for Herb to help her hang it on the wall.

When they finished, Claire told Herb to have a nice weekend.

"You too little bear, be careful of the tigers. They will get you if you are not careful."

"Oh, I will!" Claire smirked as Herb walked away. She was the tiger ready to hunt, not the other way around. *I know what I'm after, so they better watch out.*

***

After work she swung by her apartment to change into a tight peach top that with a neckline just low enough to show off her boobs, a thigh-high jean skirt, and cowboy boots. Claire threw her engagement ring into one of her top drawers, fed Tabitha, and took a shot of vodka, before she headed out to the new bar to play pool.

Walking to the bar, Claire again saw herself leaning over the pool table to take her shot when someone came up from behind her, hiked up her skirt, and gave her the ride of her life. The fantasy was so strong that Claire realized she had passed the bar and was wet in anticipation. Turning around, she resumed her walk to the bar, and the hunt was on.

The bar was great! Loud sports events played from TVs mounted across the walls, helping to drown out her crazy thoughts. Sometimes she liked to meet her friends, but on nights like this, she was a lioness out alone for the kill. The happy hour food was surprisingly good. The drinks were good too. She preferred straight hard liquor, but the fruity drinks made her look vulnerable.

She reserved a pool table and looked around for some partners.

A guy she kind of recognized came over and said, "Claire?"

"Yep, that's me."

"Mitch—from the other night."

It took her a minute and then she remembered the strange apartment and walk of shame that Sunday morning.

"Mitch!" She said, with a capital "M."

By this time, she was on her fourth drink and starting to feel good, "We should stop meeting like this. What are you doing here? "

"I got a job tending bar. I heard this place was going to be hot, so I'm working here now, actually as the head bartender. What about you?"

"I heard it was hot too," she flirted, "so I wanted to check it out." He certainly was hot. She would like to take that ride again and remember.

Claire asked, "Are you working now or can you play pool?"

"I can play pool."

And so they did, until he went on shift from midnight to 2am. They flirted and chatted like old friends, revealing normal things about their lives: where they grew up, brothers, sisters, their vocations. He was actually in engineering school, tending bar for some extra money. At some point during the night, she told him her pool table sex fantasy.

When the bar closed, he told her to stick around to take her shot. Sure enough, he made her fantasy come true, taking her from behind, pounding away the bad memories. He walked her home and she felt the familiar ache settling between her legs, knowing that tomorrow she would gladly remember the reason for the pain.

Chapter Eight

The next day, Claire woke up to the sound of stilettos running hard against her wood floor. She then realized it was Tabitha lying on her chest purring. Under normal circumstances, a cat's purr is one of her favorite sounds, often lulling her into a meditative state. But today, with her hangover, it felt like rockets going off in her head.

As gingerly as she could, she pushed Tabitha aside. After using the bathroom and swishing with mouthwash to remove that something-died–in-her-mouth taste, she went into the kitchen to pour herself a V8, to which she added a hefty shot of vodka.

Nothing like a morning pick-me-up, Claire thought as she searched around for the Extra-Strength Tylenol. *Where did I put that new super-sized bottle? Oh yea!* She checked her work bag and *thank God* it was there. She popped three, for now. She went to lie down again and Tabitha resumed her purring and this time began to knead Claire's chest like she was making bread. It wasn't quite rockets in her head anymore, but it wasn't meditative yet either.

Her ringing cell phone woke Claire up again.

"Where are you!" the overly excited shrill voice of her other best friend, Chastity, said.

"I'm at home," Claire said, *curled up in my comfy bed* thinking—*now go away*—"Where are you?"

"We are waiting for you at the restaurant to celebrate Adelynn's birthday."

OMG! Claire totally forgot and considering how she felt wasn't able or interested right now.

"Go ahead without me, I was coming down with something at work this week and it hit me hard this morning. I'm not going to make it. Tell Adelynn, 'Happy Birthday' and I will call later."

"Ok, feel better," Chastity said trying to keep the edge out of her voice as she hung up.

***

Chastity turned to the group and told them in no uncertain terms, "Claire has a hangover again! Is there anything we can do to help her, maybe we should do an intervention?"

"Maybe Chastity is right," Lexie said pouting.

"Yea," Adelynn said off-handedly, really just wanting to enjoy her birthday but knowing that she had already made a call to help with this situation.

The remaining Four Amigos, Lexie, Chastity, and Adelynn went back to cutting the cake trying to continue their celebration, knowing their friend was in trouble—big trouble.

***

Claire woke up again to the phone ringing.

"Hello gorgeous," the unfamiliar deep voice said, and before she had a chance to respond he continued, "Up for a game of pool?"

At this she laughed remembering most of last night and purred, "Good morning Mitch."

"Good morning? It's almost 4pm."

4pm? Where did the day go and is that why I'm so hungry?

"Interested in shooting pool tonight?" He asked in a sultry voice.

"Thanks, but not tonight," she said as Jeremy popped into her head; the shame starting to set in, "I have plans with some of my girlfriends," she continued, easily lying.

All she wanted to do was get some food and be left alone for the rest of the weekend to recover.

Chapter Nine

laire felt pretty good on Monday morning. She finished her coffee in the staff lounge with her coworkers and made her way to the gallery and fished out the next package which was flexible and moving.

There went her good mood, as she was again very leery about what she would uncover and discover about this piece—and herself. She really hated this artwork, this assignment, and especially this artist!

Claire gently unwrapped the piece to find a three tiered, sectional fabric wall hanging in the shape of an inverted triangle; each section balanced, held together with a gold chain, and adorned with shells and polished stones. The whole piece was suspended from a piece of driftwood, held together and attached by more gold chains. The smallest piece at the bottom of the "triangle" was a tree knot cleverly adorned with a guitar piece suspended in the center by three small gold chain pieces.

Dear Diary...I woke up this morning in a panic, feeling his hands over my mouth and hearing the water running loudly in the tub. Where was I? Not back in that bathroom on my hands and knees - the water running to cover up my screams as my brother took his fury out on me. As my head cleared, I realized that I was safe in my house, many cities away, and it was my roommate that I heard in the shower. The counselor told me that I could experience these flashbacks and that anything any time could trigger them. They will come at unexpected times she told me even many years after a traumatic event.

This flashback left me feeling again like I was in pieces. When am I going to be unafraid? Be whole? For how many years since it stopped do I have to struggle to move from victim to survivor? When I put down the drugs and alcohol, I turned to artwork; creating to push through my fears to the other side. This piece was like putting the pieces of me back together...

For the first time since curating this show, Claire felt a connection to the artist because this piece reminded her of the many pieces of herself too, held together only by a fine gold thread. There was a large piece at the top that everyone saw at work: strong, confident, smart, and diligent. The middle piece reminded Claire of the party girl who couldn't wait to find some solace in the nightlife. And the keyhole at the bottom, leading to the dark and dank life of her childhood, that Claire worked so hard to forget. *Funny how the artist didn't make a series of three this time,* Claire thought, *but there were three sections.*

Chapter Ten

As Claire turned the page of the artist's diary, she found the following poem entitled *"Web of Life."*

SPIDE —she spins her web
To catch her food
Create a home
To Survive

SPIDER—Her Web
Altered, Damaged, Destroyed

By Circumstances
Rain
The Wind
Human Intervention

SPIDER—Rebuilds her web
Recreates her home

Catches food
Survives

Again and Again
SPIDER
She weaves Her Web of Life
For Only She Knows
What it takes
To Survive
To Live to Grow

As Claire read this poem she felt herself struggling to survive, to weave her web again and again, thinking her web was in the drinking and in the men. *Do I live and grow there, or just survive?*

Chapter Eleven

On Tuesday, Claire reviewed the next piece that was unlike any she had seen in the collection so far. The artist used a fall rust colored patterned fabric and covered a number of geometric shapes made out of thick foam core board. She then assembled the shapes, securing them with glue into a cohesive, balanced piece.

As the artist continued to experiment with different structures, the collection was tied together with common elements, which included fabric, rusty hardware pieces, glass marbles, and upside down watch faces. The artist had achieved an interesting depth and shadow in this piece.

Dear Diary... I'm feeling more whole today, but not quite. Seems like the flashbacks come like hot waves, unexpected and violent, feeling like I want to explode from within. I am in an exploratory mood today still looking for new ways to put pieces of myself back together into a whole, balanced piece. I wanted to go smaller and lighter with this piece so I experimented with foam core as the foundation for my shapes, gluing the fabric flat. So instead of creating texture and patterns with sculpted fabric, I created a sculpture out of geometric pieces. The watch parts and faces continue to call to me. But no matter how hard I try, the faces always end up upside down. Like I can't move forward—stuck in time...

As Claire wrote up this piece she was reminded that she worked hard to be straight and narrow, fitting into a neat box for the whole world to see, especially at work. All the while, waiting for time to move on from that dark place, where the abuse and abandonment live.

Chapter Twelve

After lunch, Claire discovered a collection of boxes. The top of one box was collaged with sayings and then embellished with wire and one bead to resemble a spider in her web.

Dear Diary...finding these boxes at the yard sale was exhilarating—now I can use them as foundations to explore creating collages from inspirational sayings cut out of newspapers and magazines. As I collaged the top, I realized that this box is really a cry for help. If only I could lock my fears away in this box, maybe the hole in me would go away and life would be good again. I wove a spider web out of metal wire over the collage as a symbol to represent strength and courage. Expressing my need to grow away from despair and self-destruction...

As Claire picked up the box again, there was something oddly familiar about it; she had seen it somewhere—*possibly when I was little?* Before her mind could place the box, a tear slid down her cheek. Then, as she felt the hole over her own heart—deep and dark—the fear rose fast tasting like bile in her throat.

Am I self-destructing, trying to fill this hole? Where did this hole come from and why won't it go away? If I can't see it, why does it hurt so badly? How deep is it? If booze and men can't fill it, then what will?

Catching her breath, Claire went to the bathroom to wash her face and rinse her mouth. When she returned to the galley, Herb was waiting for her. Together they searched storage to see what kind of racks would best display the box collection. Satisfied with the placement of the boxes, they bid each other a good night and left the NMWA.

***

She was looking forward to her dinner with Jeremy and hopefully some warm lovemaking afterwards. Instead, when Claire returned home, all she got was a voicemail full of apologies for the many traumas he had to treat in the ER that night. *What about my traumas?*

Looking at her ring finger, she wondered where she put her engagement ring this time. *I'll find it later* Claire fumed.

With that she curled up on the couch with Tabitha, takeout Chinese, a bottle of wine, and the TV for the night.

Chapter Thirteen

It was Wednesday morning and Claire was tired with a slight hangover as she unpacked a round heavy piece. The artist used a small, antique table top to build a naturalistic scene. The background is collaged with a variety of blue tissue and rice papers to create a feeling of quiet waters. It is embellished with elements from nature including leaves, reeds, and butterfly wings giving the viewer a sense of standing at the water's edge.

Dear Diary...I decided to enter an art contest interpreting a local park. I journeyed to the park to experience, learn, and collect from her to create my collage. I had fun and excitedly submitted my artwork. Not only did I not get a prize but I didn't even make it into the show—no recognition at all!!! Being a boating area, paintings of sailboats were selected, with judges probably sticking their nose up at collages due to ignorance. Fuck those judges—I just wanted a little recognition and validation. Rejection of my artwork felt like a personal rejection of me. What was wrong with me anyway?...

There was something serene about this collage. Claire had visited this park and could relate to this piece. She wished she could have been a judge to confirm this artist's inept interpretation.

Claire's thoughts turned to validation and recognition. Was that what she was looking for and hoping to find in bed with strangers? Is that what she was really hunting for; was it validation or love, or maybe both? But did she feel "ok" the next morning, or just empty and ashamed? Was that really love, or just sex?

What was she really doing? Was it love she sought, a lust to be needed, or both? Was the sex even good since she could hardly remember the next day? And, it usually never turned into any type of relationship, and when it did, it was like she had invited her dad back into her life. That interpretation of love she didn't want, the kind that came with bruises. Spinning, Claire couldn't turn off her thoughts.

Damn this artwork, this collection, and especially the artist—fuck her! She felt that hole in her chest, wide and deep, crying for a shot of strong liquor, crying for her to run and hunt.

When Claire looked at her watch, it was quitting time—*thank God.*

***

Since it was the middle of the week, Claire headed to the gym instead of a bar. She hit the free-weights hard, then took the advanced spinning class, and then took Jose with a vengeance. She almost broke his back, riding him like a rodeo bull in their secret training room.

They did break the old weight bench and laughed until it hurt. She needed that too! Satiated and numb, she headed home.

***

After dinner, her mind started to spin again. What did she just do? Did they use a rubber? How could she be so out of control? Did she feel loved, validated? *No!* Claire could feel the internal bruising from the workout with Jose but felt more alone and sad than ever.

Her phone rang; it was Jeremy. She didn't answer it, knowing he would only offer more apologies. He was always available for strangers' emergencies, but not for someone on a daily basis that he supposedly loved.

A half hour later Chastity called and she didn't answer that either. As she stroked Tabitha, she felt drained and despondent, drinking a glass of wine to take the edge off.

Chapter Fourteen

Claire woke up late on Thursday, past the time she was to leave for work. She got up off the couch, still in her gym clothes from the previous night, and nearly tripped over an empty wine bottle.

What happened? Claire thought as her head pounded. She reached for the Extra-strength Tylenol, a shot of vodka, and the phone. Guiltily, she dialed June to call in sick. June knew she suffered from migraines and Claire hadn't called in for a while so they shouldn't suspect anything. Her boss said she would see her tomorrow and hoped she felt better. *Tomorrow was Friday! Yes!* Claire would rest up today and be ready to show up bright and sharp tomorrow. *Then,* she thought, *I have only one day until the weekend.*

***

On Friday morning back in the gallery, Claire, having recovered from her "migraine," took out a large pair of blue jeans from the collection. There was graffiti on each side. One side seemed dark and desperate. The other side depicted the artist's dreams of gaining control over her own life:

Dear Diary... I hate these jeans; they remind me of everything I don't want to be—a fat, unhappy rape victim. How did I get so big; did I think the weight would protect me? I found a box of large permanent Sharpies and decided to write away my despair. I felt drained and unsatisfied when I finished defacing my jeans and I actually hated them more with my truth spelled out for all to see. After snorting a line and taking a deep drag off a joint, I found a sense of security and an unbounding energy to take on the world. I then attacked the other side where I crafted my roadmap, where I wanted to go, where I needed to be, hoping I could draw my way into a new life...

Just holding these jeans infuriated Claire. How *is this art*? And, how *am I supposed to display this with two sides*?

At that point Shelby, one of the interns, showed up and Claire thought she probably looked like a teapot with steam coming out of her ears.

Shelby looked at the jeans and said, "Wow, they are really expressive—serious raw emotions! I love them. We are dismantling an exhibit and there are some two-sided clear cases that would work great. Let me check with Sara Marie to see if we can use one of them for your exhibit."

"Thanks," Claire said, not realizing that she had spoken her frustrations out loud. She was also glad to know that she didn't need to figure this out all by herself. *Maybe there was some artistic value in these jeans after all.*

Claire, Shelby, and Herb spent the rest of the afternoon setting up and arranging the glass case. Claire was surprised and satisfied that everything had gone smoothly. The jeans actually took on a central role for patrons to see the push-me-pull-me struggle that the artist encountered.

***

As she left work, she suddenly felt alone—all alone—as she realized that she didn't have any plans for the weekend. She sent a text to the other Four Amigos to see if they could meet her for happy hour at their favorite bar. They all texted back that they were busy with their families. This sent Claire into an immediate tailspin, reminding her that she didn't have a marriage or family to spend time with.

She couldn't remember Jeremy's schedule, so she sent him a text to see if he wanted to meet her for dinner. Three hours and a fifth of vodka later, she heard from Jeremy that he was on shift this weekend and would see her Tuesday, which was his next day off.

Spinning into oblivion, Claire spent the rest of the weekend alone with Tabitha, the bottle, and reruns, only seeing another person when they delivered food.

Chapter Fifteen

Monday morning found Claire despondent as she trekked to work, stopping at the local Starbucks for their strongest brew and three espresso shots for good measure. She took it black and hoped it would activate her fast. Placing a fake, warm smile on her face, she greeted her coworkers and headed to the gallery.

The next piece in the collection was a representational collage depicting "The Fool" from the Tarot deck. The artist created it with torn-up journal entries, fabric, and found objects... The ripped journal pages were cryptic, as if to say, *I know what I did to walk off the ledge, fool that I am.*

Dear Diary...I joined a group of wayward artists each with their own unique style that is anything but traditional. We all live in or near water communities, but none of us paint sailboats, which is why our work didn't sell that well. Not to say that it wasn't great art—just not representational—which some people just couldn't wrap their minds around. Together we supported each other through our own shows, while educating our communities about the full depth and potential of art. Attempting to teach that, in addition to providing beautiful scenes, artwork is an expression of life, helping the artist to move in and through life situations; healing one brush stroke at a time.

For one of our shows, we decided to each pick a card to depict from the Tarot. I chose The Fool because he was so recklessly certain that he could walk off that cliff with no consequence. This was the first time I was challenged with a representational piece to collage. What I most enjoyed was figuring out how to depict the symbolism inert in the card—I enjoyed tearing up my journal writings to glue down as a background on the pre-stretched canvas. Then I built my interpretation on top. I stiffened fabric for the tree and added plastic flowers for brightness. I used sea glass to represent the rocky edge and a real doll as the fool. As I created this piece, I reflected on many of my reckless choices only to discover that they were always met with an equally negative consequence...

As Claire read the artist's diary she unexpectedly fell in love with this piece. She wasn't really into Tarot cards, but she looked up "The Fool" and felt an immediate connection, appreciating the artist's interpretation. She especially loved how clearly "The Fool" was depicted walking off the cliff without a second look back.

This reminded Claire of her nightlife. She walked off that cliff every time she sat at the bar, pulled a drink to her lips and felt the liquid slide down her throat, heating her up with its glow. How her prowess took over, looking for that perfect man to jump off the cliff with her. Were there any consequences she needed to be concerned about? She was just having fun and living the party life, right? Claire went home that night still contemplating "The Fool," going to bed early without a drink or a man.

Chapter Sixteen

Claire woke up the next day refreshed, more so than she could remember. She was actually looking forward to going to work to see what the next piece of artwork had in store for her. She also remembered that it was Tuesday and Jeremy was coming over later tonight.

The next piece Claire examined was a glass vase. It had a three-dimensional water scene created with stiffened blue rice paper to create waves which flowed around the vase. Within the water, the artist had tucked colorful glass fish. When she was done unpacking this box, Claire had a collection of eight vases, each with a distinct personality determined by the types and colors of paper the artist wove together, as well as the items she chose for added embellishment.

Dear Diary...I continued to do shows with my group of women artists—without a single sale. My frustration grew and it was recommended that I make something functional. Defeated, I did. I took my abstract collages and put them on vases. Instead of fabric, I used paper. I enjoyed collecting all sorts of paper, glass vases, chains, beads, and other found objects. Like a manufacturing factory, I make these vases while trying to express myself creatively. True to the suggestion, I sold quite a lot of these vases and even got them into some prominent galleries around town...

While Claire liked the vases and would even enjoy having one in her apartment, she also felt sad that the artist had to bend herself and her creativity around a functional piece to please others. She actually started to understand the need for an artist to express themselves, allowing them to dig through the dreadful, dark pain in order to let go and move through to the light.

Claire wondered if all artists really knew or understood what they were expressing, discovering? As an art curator, Claire observed art as an outsider, using her art history background to hang a show and educate the audience. The studio work she did in college was technical, providing Claire only with the necessary foundation to understand the works of art she would curate.

Claire realized that studying this art collection gave her a new insight into art as a necessary means of expression. It made her contemplate returning to the studio to push beyond the technical and into her own creative expression.

***

In preparation for her evening with Jeremy, Claire picked up their favorite Indian food on her way home. She eventually found her engagement ring and settled it back on her finger. She couldn't wait for the sex, but even more to feel safe and secure in his arms.

Well she did wait, for over an hour, nursing a couple glasses of wine. The food turned cold and so did Claire's heart as tears slipped into her wine glass. Jeremy finally sent a text to say that he was called into the ER to deal with victims from a major accident. Her disappointment and anger soared as she felt abandoned once again; she threw her ring back into the drawer.

Chapter Seventeen

Claire was in a foul mood on Wednesday morning. Her period was late. *It was never late.* She was glad for the distraction of work and the next discovery. After a strong cup of coffee and a huge pastry, Claire attacked her day.

As she made her way through the next box, she realized this was another three-piece series. *Back to that,* she spat to herself. Each piece featured a distinct tree, created from stiffened colored paper laid upon a different background.

There was a short, sturdy, red tree anchored on top of a yellow and orange, circular, woven background representative of a brilliant sun.

There was a proud, blue tree sitting alone in a landscape theme with flat, glass pieces for leaves.

Claire's favorite was the tall, black tree against a stark, white background. It reminded her of the winter and how one could see through the forest to the mysteries hidden by summer foliage.

Dear Diary...I still have a box of torn up journal entries from "The Fool," so I decided to use them as the first layer of this next series. Today I am creating trees because yesterday I saw some very large, old trees that emulated strength and wisdom. Anxious for a connection and to absorb what those trees had, I tried to hug them, but their circumference was beyond the circle of my arms. I need to know how they plant their roots deep into the soil to grow big and strong in order to withstand Mother Nature's elements, especially strong winds and torrential rains. Again, I need to create three pieces, each a different interpretation of a tree.

Using the torn up journal pages is symbolic of the past that does not exist anymore, fertilizing the soil for my much needed new roots. How many times did I write the same cry for help? Over and over I captured the self-hatred and loathing, as I could not drown my sorrows deep enough to make me forget. With each tree I create, I am planting new roots, deeper and deeper, to heal and grow through the pain of my past storms...

Despite herself, Claire felt a connection to these pieces—to the artist. The trees felt strong and rooted, like she wanted to be. Yet, seeing pieces of the diary peeking through, she could feel the vulnerability of the artist, her vulnerability— *could I really be pregnant*? At that moment, Claire's boss stopped by.

"Hi Claire, how is everything going?" June asked as she looked around at the developing exhibition.

"Good," Claire said, "I am about half way through the collection."

As June took her time reading the write-ups, Claire felt her chest tighten, finding it hard to get enough air for a full breath.

June finally spoke, "The hanging order looks good. There is a nice flow and I especially like the use of the jeans in the dual sided Plexiglas display case."

"Thanks to our intern, Shelby, who helped to arrange for the case," Claire spat out.

June wasn't done, "Claire, you need to do more work on the write-ups. While they are technically correct about the color, texture and placement of items within the collages, I need you to remember that this is an exhibit about *Art and Healing*. I need you to move beyond the technical and dig deep to write about the healing the artist experienced from creating each piece. Did you find the diaries?"

"Yes." Claire said; throat dry, eyes moist.

"Good!" June said, "They should help you to rewrite the descriptions for the wall and catalog."

With that June was gone. She had blown through like a tornado, leaving Claire to realize that her roots were not planted well enough to withstand some basic constructive criticism and direction.

Claire wasn't sure how to "dig deep." Feeling the storm clouds gathering, she would think about that later.

Right now, I need a drink, but isn't alcohol a big no-no for a pregnant woman? While she was still contemplating that drink, her phone rang. It was Jeremy. He had a night off and wanted to come over.

The sun peaked through the clouds and she said, "Sure, see ya soon."

***

On her way out of the NMWA, she stopped by the Madonna and Child painting. While the painting brought her home to a place of warmth and safety, it also stirred up a whirlwind in her belly that mirrored the fear she felt about having a baby.

Could she be like the Madonna, able to provide a loving home? Would her baby be safe—from her; her family's history? Who was the father? Could she pass the baby off as Jeremy's? Could she live with a lie—forever—if the baby wasn't Jeremy's? The questions flew at her like golf balls off a driving range.

***

On her way home, she ordered Thai takeout. While waiting at the bar, she downed a glass of deep red wine. Feeling more relaxed, she headed home. Once home, her heart started to pound hard as she remembered that she needed her engagement ring.

"There you are," she exclaimed as she slipped it on her ring finger, just minutes before Jeremy showed up. Dinner was good, accompanied by wine and conversation, with each catching the other up on their lives since the last time they met.

After making slow and soft love, Claire lying satiated in his arms whispered, "Jeremy, have you ever thought about how big a family you would want?"

"Sure," he said, "A big one. As an only child, I want my kids to have other kids to play with, fight with and grow up with. Just not right now. I barely have time to pop a frozen dinner into the microwave or see you. My dream of a large family can't start until I'm settled into an internal medicine practice with set hours, once my ER residency ends in a couple of years. What about you?"

Claire—ashamed—had not told Jeremy about her tumultuous childhood.

"A large family sounds good," she laughed. Claire visualized a family in a large kitchen, around a big island, with normal chaos and commotion. Everyone was trying to get their day started or sitting down after a long day, sharing their challenges and successes.

As her fantasy ended, she realized that Jeremy was snoring. She snuck out of bed for another glass of wine, rinsing away the dream. Then she cried herself softly to sleep.

Chapter Eighteen

Claire woke up the next day with a knot in her belly and fog in her head. And Jeremy was gone! *Where was Jeremy*, she thought bitterly? In the kitchen she found a note that read,

"Sorry had to leave. Got paged to the hospital, LU."

The family fantasy from the night before evaporated as quickly as steam from a cup of coffee.

Claire showered, fed the cat, and still—*no period*. On her way to work she thought *I need to buy a pregnancy test*. But right now, what Claire really needed was to talk to someone. She knew that the other Four Amigos were not a smart bet since they were all very family friendly. Maybe she could reach Evi, her oldest friend, who was a 5'4" beautiful, exotic mix of an Asian mother and African American father. It had been a while, but Claire went through something like this with Evi in their teens, *so Evi should understand—right?*

As she waited for her Venti—triple espresso coffee, Claire sent a text to Evi that she needed to talk as soon as possible. Due to the time difference in Hawaii, Claire knew she would have to be patient as she waited for a return call. As Claire continued her walk to work she thought, *I don't think caffeine is good for babies. Fuck it, I need it.*

Entering work, Claire made her normal greetings. She was sure that her professional outfit and beautiful smile hid the rage boiling silently below the surface.

***

The next piece was a sculpted collage on foam core that featured a paper sculpture material that secured a fan shell. The artist used two pieces of driftwood that crossed at the bottom and wire to frame and secure the collage. It formed an upside-down triangle; the alchemical symbol of for water.

Interesting, Claire thought, *all of the objects were found at the beach and in the water.* She wondered if the artist did that on purpose.

Dear Diary...I have just returned from collecting driftwood, shells and fossils from the shores of Flags Pond in Calvert County, Maryland, some of which are over 60 million years old. Amazing! I am pumped, and my artistic coffers are overflowing. I am ready to explore building sculptural, three-dimensional artwork that addresses pieces of me that don't fit together, but can somehow be unified. The driftwood is especially appealing; as I wonder how long it took for the rough edges to wear smooth by the constant massaging of the surf. I also wonder how long it will take for the hard edges of my self-hatred and self-destruction to wear away, how much creating does it take to heal?...

Claire was taken aback by the artist's questions; opening the flood gates for her own questions: How many generations of Sebastians did it take for her father to turn out the way he was? Was he beaten as a boy, screamed at by an angry father, unprotected by a meek, unavailable mother? Or was it his mother who was angry and abusive, or both?

Claire wondered how her mom became meek, cowering in the corner of her room when all hell broke out around her. Why didn't she stand up and protect herself and her children? Why did her mom morph into a mouse? Was it to protect herself? Claire wondered if her mom didn't want anyone to know she was around, so she couldn't get into trouble, get punished, and get whipped.

As tears slipped down Claire's cheeks, she wondered whether she was destined to carry on this tradition, the wreckage of her parent's past or was there a way to stop these patterns before she could even think about bringing a baby into her world? Is there a body of water big enough to wash her clean of all those past injustices and prime a new canvas for which to recreate her on? Remembering that she was at work, she quickly wiped her tears away.

Herb showed up with a box of tissues for Claire, who was surprised to see that it was already 4:30pm. She didn't remember stopping to eat lunch and wondered where the day had gone. They hung the artwork, locked the gallery, and left for the evening.

***

As Claire made her way to the front door of the NMWA, her phone rang. *It was Evi!*

"Hey Sis," Claire answered as she walked outside. "Sis" was an enduring term they picked up long ago to indicate their special, sister-like relationship.

"Hi Sis," Evi said, "so glad to get your text. Perfect timing! I was just getting ready to text you too! I'm on my way home! I'm done with active duty and moving back to D.C."

"OMG," Claire yelped, "I'm so glad. I have really been missing you."

It had been years since the girls had seen each other; each going their own way after high school to pursue their own dreams. Like all good friends, they kept in touch by email, texts, and other social media for all the important dates.

Sometimes there was an occasional visit if Evi came back to the area between deportations.

"Can I help you move? Do you have somewhere to stay? Do you want to bunk with me?" Claire's questions came fast and furious, momentarily making her forget about her own problem.

"I would love to crash with you for a while," Evi said. She continued offhandedly, "Is there an elevator in the building? I have a lot of stuff to move and don't do steps that well anymore"

"Yes, we have an elevator," Claire said absently. She was so excited she had almost forgotten why she sent the earlier text.

"Claire," Evi's voice grew serious, "what's going on?"

Claire knew it was no use to beat around the bush with Evi. They had been through and seen too much together as kids; they could read each other like books.

Standing in front of the pharmacy and holding tightly to her tears, Claire softly said, "Evi—I think I'm pregnant. It's late and I'm never late. I am going into the store in a minute to buy a test box or two," Claire laughed a little sardonically. She knew that if she got a positive result, she would want to pee on a number of strips just to make certain.

Evi said, "Ok, I'm here for you. Whatever you need, decide, I will be by your side. Text or call me when you know for sure, and I will see you this weekend."

***

As Evi hung up, she hoped that her voice sounded steady and supportive when she told Claire that she was there for her. She knew Claire's history with partying and men—lots of men—and knew this could be a very difficult situation.

As she reached for her prosthetic leg, Evi knew that she too was dealing with a life altering situation and hoped that Claire would be there for her; would still love and accept her—whole or not.

Chapter Nineteen

Claire hung up with Evi and made a left into the Irish bar for some courage before she could even think about going into the pharmacy. *I know I shouldn't drink, but until I take the test, I'm not really pregnant, am I?*

"Hey Claire," the bartender/owner said, "looking good after a long day of work, the regular?"

"Not today Tommie, give me a double shot of vodka, neat."

As she threw back her drink like water, Tommie told her he had some new wine in the cellar. She looked coyly at him and said, "I've been looking for a new wine."

As he led Claire down the ancient, narrow, wood steps into the basement wine cellar, he shouted over his shoulder, "Sheila, cover the counter!"

"It's been a long time Claire."

"Too long," Claire replied, huskily.

As he closed the door, Claire deposited her hose and panties on the ground. He then lifted her up onto crates of wine stacked against the back wall. He hiked her skirt up and between passionate kisses entered her.

At first he was gentle, finding his way into the depths of her wetness. Claire didn't want gentle. So she encouraged him by scooting down, positioning her hips and knees higher, pumping him faster. He got the message and met her fury until she came in a mind numbing rush, her scream muffled by his mouth covering hers.

It took them both a long moment to come down off their high and compose themselves.

"Don't forget the new wine," Claire giggled.

Exhausted, he said, "Claire, stop by again next week. I'm expecting a shipment of new exotic wines from Virginia."

"From Virginia?" Claire laughed a little sardonically, "I might just be in the mood for exotic."

Carrying the newest wine, they made their way back upstairs and he poured her a glass to try. She downed it like she was drowning.

"Wow that is good!" Claire exclaimed, "I'll take a few bottles."

She paid her bill and headed out.

***

Despite her buzz from the alcohol and unyielding fuck, she was hit by a blast of cold reality and remembered to head into the pharmacy. Each box held two test strips, so she bought two boxes, from different companies. She then picked up some Chinese takeout to go with her new wine.

After she had finished dinner, she peed on the first test strip. Those two minutes felt like hours—*pink*. She opened the other box and peed on that test strip—*a big plus sign*. She peed on another test strip—*pink*. *Third time is the charm* she thought, and didn't pee on the remaining strip.

Claire tried to call Evi to confirm her predicament, but when she didn't get an answer, she sent a text to Evi. She would have left a voicemail, but that seemed too real; a text not so real.

Evi sent a text back telling her to hang in there, that she was traveling, and they could talk about it when she got to D.C. sometime tomorrow afternoon. Claire shot off a quick return text to tell Evi where to find the spare key in case she wasn't home when she got there.

Claire hastily cleaned up the guest bedroom for Evi as she finished a bottle of wine and went to bed without a second thought on what to do next.

Chapter Twenty

Claire woke up in a haze, her head pounding. She found the vodka bottle in the freezer on the way to the bathroom and took a long swig to start her day.

This is the last time I am going to start my day off with a drink, she thought. *Who does that? It's a work day and I can't afford to be drunk.*

"But I am not drunk," she said out loud to Tabitha, "Just ready and steady to face the day." As she wondered why she needed to "face the day," Claire could have sworn the cat was looking at her with a questioning smirk on her face.

What was wrong with today that she couldn't face? Claire loved her job and was even getting into the *Art and Healing* collection. Starting her shower, she saw the two pink sticks and one "+" stick, and it all came back to her—she was pregnant. Her romp with Tommie also resurfaced. *Jesus, what was I thinking?*

She stepped into the shower. Despite the warm water, she felt cold and alone. How did she get herself into this situation? It used to be a different guy every month or at least every couple of weeks. When did she start having sex in the middle of the week with strangers?

Well, Tommie wasn't really a stranger; she had been a regular at his bar since she moved to D.C. after college. They had made the trip to the wine cellar a number of times over the years. At first it was fun, every couple of months. *But now it was just—just what?*

Something she needed to do? What was she looking for? Did they use protection? She started to laugh and cry at the same time. Protection for what, she was pregnant. She almost forgot about diseases, like Aids. Oh yeah, she thought bitterly, protection from that, too! She couldn't remember the last time she fucked Tommie, so didn't know if the baby was his.

She didn't know whose it was, and there were at least three guys that could be the father. The movie, *Three Men and A Baby* popped into her head and she started to cry harder. Of course, she was only a child when that movie came out in 1987, but Aunt Jo watched it over and over again, so Claire knew it well. This was not Hollywood, and Tom Selleck, Steve Guttenberg, nor Ted Danson would rescue her. Despite the clean smell of the shower gel lathered on her body, she felt dirty.

Chapter Twenty-One

As soon as Claire arrived that Friday morning, June was waiting for her, reviewing the show.

"Do you have the updated cards for me to review?"

Good morning to you too! Claire thought. Her headache started to resurface.

"I'm still working on them," Claire lied as easily as she slept with men she didn't care about.

Where did that come from? She thought.

"Please have them on my desk by COB Monday," June said and walked out.

Now it felt like hurricane Katrina was settling between her ears. Claire gathered all the cards off the wall, found the diary and her notes and headed to the employee lounge for another coffee. There she ran into Shelby, who started to chat her up. At first all Claire heard was *blablablabla*.

Then she heard Shelby say, "The curator I usually work with isn't in, so I'm not sure what I'm going to do today."

"How are your writing skills?" Claire heard herself say.

"Great!" chirped Shelby, "My double major is English and Art History, with a little psychology thrown in. I'm considering a major in art therapy, but wanted to see what the curator world was like since art therapy doesn't pay much, and curating keeps me close to the art world."

TMI thought Claire. But then she realized what she had here—passion, writing, and energy—things she was definitely missing today.

"Shelby, how would you like to help me catalogue the *Art and Healing* exhibit? I need to update these cards," Claire said, pointing to the stack on the table, "Right now they are technical, and they need to talk more to the emotions and healing behind each piece. How the artist used each piece to understand her challenges, and because of expressing herself through artwork, how she digested the challenge and grew." Claire felt like she was rambling, but was surprised at how much clarity she had around this exhibit.

"Wow!" Shelby yipped loudly, sending a thunder clap through Claire's brain, and then finished with a louder, cheerier "Absolutely!"

Yippee Claire thought, wanting to throw up. Not sure from this conversation or—*Oh Shit—maybe from morning sickness—so soon?* She excused herself, saying she would be right back. Claire quickly made her way to the bathroom and threw up. She used the mouthwash in her purse and headed back to Shelby, feeling much better.

She was going to dump the whole assignment on Shelby, but thought better of it. This was her show and her career so she decided to work with her instead. When she returned, she found Shelby reading through the cards and was glad to hear her say, "These look good!"

Claire suggested they go up to the library and grab one of the private conference rooms. Once settled, they used the software designed for gallery cataloguing. Reviewing the technical write-up card, picture of the artwork and the artist's diary, Shelby updated each card, weaving in what the artist felt and how much, if any, she had healed. Claire reviewed each card, making some editorial changes before moving on to the next. They had a nice flow going. By the end of the day, they had finished all the cards.

They returned to the gallery to number and sorted the cards according to the order of the artwork. Claire thanked Shelby and asked her if she would be available around her other work to finish with the cards.

Shelby replied, "Yes!"

Claire had a good sense of leadership and directed the rest of the process. Claire would continue to review the pieces, hang them, draft the technical write-up, and then schedule another day to meet with Shelby for the healing piece. Claire was pretty proud of herself, and they headed their separate ways for lunch.

Chapter Twenty-Two

After lunch, Claire returned to the gallery to find only two pieces in the next series. The artist included a large leaf and foliage as the focus in both of these very red collages. The red paint was energetically applied in a Van Gogh-like style across the entire background, engulfing the central leaves. Yellow-gold paint adorned one of the paintings creating a motion around the piece, forcing the viewer's eye to try to focus on the subject while getting caught in the directional motion of the brush strokes.

Perhaps the artist was trying to focus on herself and wasn't quite there yet.

Dear Diary...I started to collect leaves, and other interesting items discarded by nature to incorporate into my pieces. I also am exploring how to import the positive words within my collage in order to honor myself and my light. Not sure why I am drawn to these leaves, but I love the large—intact ones—that have survived the fall.

I am in a relationship where my partner is not supportive of my involvement with the Women About Art Group. Funny how the acronym is WAAG, like we wag our finger at snobs who can only appreciate art that looks like something they recognize, versus those that can appreciate its value for expressive adventure. That includes my partner, for he is critical and uninterested. It is exciting to be part of this group of very creative women and trying to bond with them. But, on the other hand, it is despairing and disheartening to be in a relationship that is one-sided and creates a lot of negative energy around trying to find my creative passion.

Not sure how to let that go or reconcile it, so I do the only thing I know how, I create to move through it! When I am wound up like this; I love to paint—fast and furious. Being in this mood, the only color that satisfies me is red, I quickly and violently paint the canvas with a large flat brush, creating a thick textured river for the background. I attached the large leaf and foliage as the central character. Then I added words that inspired me, told me who I was, wanted to be. I watered down the acrylic paint with gel medium and painted a softer transparent coat of red on top of the leaf to blend everything together. On only one piece, I added some gold to represent the brief brilliance I sometimes recognize as myself...

These paintings made Claire feel uncomfortable. The single leaf reminded Claire of the child in her womb; the need for a drink rose unexpectedly. Not today she thought I am not taking a drink today! She decided to engage in an intense, spinning class at the gym instead. She hoped Jose wasn't there since she wasn't sure if she could control that urge either.

Turning her attention back to the artwork and focusing on the artist's diary, she wondered if she could find her brilliance, her rainbow through the storm of this pregnancy. *What a mess*, she thought. She had always wanted kids to right the wrongs of her family's past and make up for the love and security that she did not receive. *Did her need for love get her into this mess?* She wondered. *How many men have I been with that could be this baby's father?*

She didn't think that she could keep this baby. She wouldn't even have a clue about who its father was until it came out, and she could see its features. Oh, and she almost forgot about her fiancé Jeremy. Why did she make that commitment? Did she really love Jeremy or the fact that he wasn't that available? Or was she in love with being in love?

Her head and fury were spinning like a two funneled tornado. She rushed to the bathroom to throw up again. *Definitely morning sickness*, she thought.

After she had composed herself, Claire made her way to June's office, happy for the distraction. She greeted the administrative assistant and asked if June was available.

A minute later, she said, "Sure, go on in."

"Hi," Claire said as she handed the stack of cards to June, "I worked with Shelby, and we updated the cards to include the *Art and Healing* angle."

"Great!" June said. I will look them over and get them back to you next week. And, Claire, thanks for getting to this as promptly as you did, I appreciate it. We are under a lot of pressure to open this show on time, and I want to keep everything on track."

"I understand," Claire said, sensing this was an apology, which she graciously accepted, "Shelby and I will be working together as we hang the rest of the show to deliver the write-ups as requested. Please let me know if there is anything else that you need. See you on Monday."

"Goodnight and have a nice weekend," June said, absently.

Chapter Twenty-Three

When Claire left work, she headed to a small Italian Restaurant near her apartment to meet Evi for some dinner and drink some wine to unwind. She didn't think having a glass or two of wine as drinking because she had heard on WTOP, D.C.'s top news radio station, that a glass of wine each day was good for something. She wished she could remember what, but all she knew was that wine helped keep something in the body healthy.

She was going to head over to Tommie's bar for some corned beef and cabbage and remembered that Evi loved Italian food. Plus she wanted a quiet place with no temptations to talk to Evi. So she sent a text to Evi to meet her for dinner once she was ready.

***

When Evi got Claire's text, she was in the apartment dropping off her stuff, which consisted of her large duffle bag. She found her room warm and cozy, the cat curled up on the bed. She and Claire always loved Aunt Jo's cats; they were fun to play with and a great distraction from the everyday terrors that they both experienced. She played with the cat for a while and got lost in the purring until she remembered the text and headed to the restaurant to meet Claire.

It was dark now, but the city was abuzz with lots of people walking and winding down from their week. Evi had a short two block walk. She was pretty comfortable with her prosthetic leg after all the therapy and felt secure with that distance.

She missed Hawaii, but she loved D.C. too. Everything she wanted and enjoyed was close and available, including the VA hospital where she would need to visit more often than not, remembering that she was one of the lucky ones. As Evi walked along slowly, she passed homeless on the street corners, no doubt that some were also wounded warriors and not so lucky in that they couldn't or wouldn't cope with the reality of post-war back in the states. She wanted to stop and counsel them, give them money, but she knew that until they asked, she couldn't promote the alternative and could also not support their addictions.

Sometimes she would drop off care packages of food and other necessities. But not tonight—she was on another mission to see her oldest and dearest friend—who had asked for her help. Because of Claire's cry for help, Evi did feel justified to be there for Claire, she just had to be careful not to try to fix everything, because she wanted to rescue people. She was not sure where that came from, but that is how she ended up going into the army as a medic.

Coming back to reality, Evi was glad she was getting closer; her leg was getting sore. She was excited to see Claire, but a little scared about sharing her own secret. She knew they would be distracted for a while with the baby situation, but not for that long. As she neared the alley just before the restaurant, she heard someone crying and gasping. At the same time, she got a text with one simple word, "Help!"

Oh my God, it was Claire, Evi just knew it. Her medic training kicked in, and she forgot all about the pain in her leg. "Claire!" she yelled, loud enough to scare anyone away.

"Over here," Claire cried back softly.

The light from the back of the restaurant illuminated a slumped figure on the ground and something wet, a lot of wet. As she got closer, the strong metallic smell told Evi that it was blood. She saw that Claire was sitting in a pool of blood—*too much blood!* Looking around, she also noticed that someone had left a bloody handprint on the partially opened restaurant back door.

She took out her cell phone and called 911, giving the operator the address and situation. Having dealt with many traumatized veterans with war wounds, she knew that now was not the time for questions. The police would be all over Claire with that soon enough. She was just here to help and keep Claire calm until transport, or rather, the ambulance got her.

"I'm here," Evi repeated over and over, wanting desperately to hold and hug her, but knowing that she might contaminate the crime scene. *The crime scene*, she thought, *Claire was a crime scene. What the hell had happened here?*

Evi had recently heard that D.C. emergency response was challenged due to an aging fleet of vehicles, many in disrepair. She said a prayer for a quick response and she heard sirens sooner than she thought possible.

In her most professional, yet soothing voice, Evi told her, "I'll be right back Claire. You are ok, and I am going to bring help."

She waited at the entrance to the alley and waived in the first responders. They quickly went to work assessing the situation. The police sealed off the scene and started to ask Evi questions. She told them what she found when she got there, pointing them to the bloody handprint. Evi tried to stay out of their way as they stabilized Claire and loaded her onto a gurney. But she was close enough to hear rape. *Raped? No, No, No!* Evi thought, *not now, not again.* Her own memories rushed up to meet her, and she almost fainted from the pain.

She looked that fear square in the eyes and said aloud, "Not now," with an inner strength she didn't know she possessed but for which she was grateful. Evi did, however, know where the power behind the courage came from, and she looked up, smiled, and wiped a single tear away.

"Are you pregnant," one of the EMTs asked Claire.

"Yes," Claire whispered, "I just found out this week."

"Ok, you are going to be ok," the EMT continued.

Evi caught the look she passed to her partner, knowing what that pool of blood meant. As the EMTs were loading Claire into the ambulance, Evi asked to ride along. At first they protested saying that only family could come along. Evi whispered about her wounded warrior status and told them that she was Claire's family—her step-sister. Evi sat down on the cold bench, taking Claire's hand as her sister, glad to step out of her medic role.

***

When they arrived at the hospital, the police's rape counselor, Beverly, walked Claire through the procedure. Evi thought, it's not bad enough being raped, but now you become an object of dissection.

"Can she stay with me?" Claire pleaded pointing quickly at Evi adding, "She's my step-sister."

"Ok," Beverly said, "but she needs to sit over there out of the way until we finish."

Claire slowly let go of Evi's hand crying, "Ok, ok."

Beverly more softly now said, "Claire, I know this is not pleasant, but we need to collect evidence, have the doctor perform a complete physical, and get as much information from you as possible now."

Evi observed that just like on TV, the nurse took out the rape kit, cut off her clothes, bagged them up, and proceeded to collect evidence from every orifice in Claire's body, including what was under her fingernails. They took pictures of bruises that were forming on Claire's body, especially her stomach area where it looked like someone had repeatedly punched her. Her wrists also showed signs of trauma, where someone tried to restrain her.

"All right Claire," Beverly said, "We are almost done, just some questions, ok?"

"Yes," whimpered Claire, breaking Evi's heart.

Beverly preceded, "Claire can you tell us what happened?"

Chapter Twenty-Four

Claire began, "I was in the Italian Restaurant having a glass of wine waiting for my step-sister, Evi, when I headed to the bathroom in the back. The next thing I know there was someone behind me, saying 'Bitch, you want it now? It's either me or this knife,' and he pushed me out the back door where he started to punch me in the stomach. I was fighting back, I think I scratched him. I heard the knife drop when he knocked my head against the cement wall and then tied my hands tight with something to hold them above my head. He hiked up my skirt."

Claire gasped for air, "He said, 'You always were such a pretty girl, everyone's favorite,' and he forced himself inside me. 'It's been too long, way too long.'"

He had his other hand over my mouth so I couldn't scream. I started to cramp up. He finished and went back into the bar. When I looked down, I saw the blood."

"Did you recognize him? Did you see his face?" Beverly asked.

"He seemed familiar," Claire said, "It was dark, but I am not sure how much of his face I saw. I was scared, so I shut my eyes to shut him out. But when I did open them I could see from his hands that he was white."

She took a breath and then said, "He also had a crooked nose." She stopped and sniffed, like she remembered a smell.

"Did you smell something?" Beverly queried.

"Smelled like oil, like a car mechanic," Claire answered. Flashing back to another time when her father's brother—a mechanic—put his hands on her. She would never forget that smell. Never date or get that close to a car mechanic again. *Oh, it couldn't be,* she thought, *No, no, no! Not her crazy fucking uncle, no he was dead from a drunken car accident.*

Oh My God, his son—her cousin—Junior. Where did he come from? She started to cry almost choking as she gasped for air. She thought she recognized that voice.

"Evi!" She cried loudly, "Junior, I think it was Junior." Repeating, "Jesus Christ," over and over again like a mantra to try to heal the wound, "When is this going to end?"

Evi was up in a minute holding and rocking Claire, telling her everything was going to be okay.

Beverly gently said, "Claire, who is Junior?"

Claire seemed to go into shock as her eyes glazed over, and her voice changed to that of a child's, "My father's, brother's son. My fucking cousin."

"His father—my uncle—used to touch me when I was little with those dirty mechanic hands. No one did anything, no one did anything."

Claire's voice was rising, "I tried to tell them, my mommy and daddy, and they didn't listen, they didn't believe me. The only way for me to escape was for me to go over to Aunt Jo's house when I saw him coming. She and Evi were my real family."

The nurse came into to give Claire a sedative and Evi jumped up and said, "No! She has been drinking; there might be a bad reaction. Plus, I don't think knocking her out is the answer."

"Claire, what is Junior's full name?" Beverly asked.

Claire looked at the nurse and said, "No sedatives! I want to be clear to end this once and for all." She seemed to discover a fight within her that was formidable.

"Ok," the nurse replied, "but we do need to give you antibiotics that are standard in this type of situation."

"Ok," Claire spat out.

Claire gave Beverly Junior's full name and told her where he lived in Baltimore when she left to live in D.C.

Chapter Twenty-Five

As Beverly was finishing up, Jeremy came into the room. "Claire?"

"Jeremy?" cried Claire, reaching for his hand.

He took her hand and said, "Yes, honey, I'm here. But, I have to let Dr. Ashbury exam you since I can't treat family.

"Hi Jeremy, I'm Evi. I'm glad to meet you finally, but sorry it's under these circumstances."

"Hi Evi, what happened?" he said between gritted teeth.

"Rape," was all Evi could spit out.

Jeremy excused himself when Dr. Ashbury arrived. She introduced herself to Claire. She was the on call GYN doctor and psychologist with a specialization in rape victims.

She performed the examination that also included an ultrasound. She was very kind but very professional.

Dr. Ashbury told Claire that she would be right back. Claire saw her stop to talk to Jeremy and shake her head. She thought she saw tears in Jeremy's eyes as he turned to go to his next patient.

Dr. Ashbury returned and told Claire, "I am sorry to inform you that you lost the baby." Hesitating for only a moment, she continued, "Since you were not that far along, I don't think we need to do a D and C, but I will want to hold you until Sunday morning to make a final determination. Ok?"

Claire looking at Evi and barely breathing, cried, "Why Sunday? "I want to go home now!"

Dr. Ashbury responded calmly, "We are going to keep you until Sunday to do a few more tests and monitor you for any internal bleeding."

Claire said, "Ok," a tear sliding down her face. She wasn't sure if she was relieved about the baby or sad because it was now not her choice, but she would think about that tomorrow. Right now, she wanted to get cleaned up.

"When can I take a shower?" Claire demanded a little too loudly.

Dr. Ashbury smiled and said, "Shortly, as soon as we find you a room. Is there someone that can bring you some clean clothes to wear home?"

All of a sudden Claire looked panic stricken. "Where is my purse?" She cried.

Evi said, "I have it." Claire relaxed as Evi continued, "They found it in the alley. It looks like everything is in there, your wallet, cell phone, and keys. After they processed it, they dropped it off a little while ago."

"Ok, ok," Claire said. "Evi, can you help me and give them my medical cards. Then go home and feed the cat, get some rest, and grab me something to wear for tomorrow, sweats or something like that?"

***

Evi was glad to help, especially since she felt helpless. She always felt helpless where Claire was concerned. Maybe that is why she became a medic; maybe that is where that came from. Every time Claire came over to Aunt Jo's, which was often; she was running, always running from someone or something, sometimes bloody.

All Evi wanted to do was take the pain away, make the mean people stop hurting Claire. She recently learned that she was powerless over mean people, but she could still help victims to heal, to become survivors. She could be a messenger.

In her line of work, she helped wounded warriors. Today, she was sent to help Claire on her journey from victim to survivor. This was a journey which actually did not start today, it started more than 20 years ago, when they were both little.

"Anything you need," Evi said, "I love you and am here to help for as long as you need me."

Once Claire got to a room, showered, and was settled in bed, Evi left about midnight to go to her new home.

Chapter Twenty-Six

Late the next morning, the police stopped by the hospital to ask Claire some more questions and show her a six pack of pictures. She told them she hadn't seen Junior in at least 10 years since they were teenagers. But she definitely recognized him in one of the photos as the man who attacked and raped her. His crooked nose was a medal he wore from a fight with his dad.

One of the cops said, "We picked him up on a surveillance tape outside the bar leaving in a van. One of the restaurant's catering vans broke down in Baltimore and was towed to where Junior worked. He fixed it and was delivering it. He was collecting his money when the bartender said he saw you sitting at the bar and got a weird look on his face. The bartender then saw him follow you to the bathroom in the back, but didn't think anything of it."

"After the uhhh, incident," he continued, "Junior tried to escape in that van. He was flying down the Baltimore/Washington Parkway toward Baltimore, but was intercepted and chased by Prince George's County police. The van flipped over a guard rail and he couldn't be revived."

Continuing he said, "So ma'am, if you're sure that was him, he is gone, he died from the crash. You are safe from him now."

Claire mumbled, "Dead. Safe. Ok, thank you."

The cops left and Claire continued to mumble to herself. *Junior is dead just like his father. Dead means you both can't touch me anymore. But what does 'safe' really mean? Am I safe from painful memories that won't die? Dead or alive, I still come from a fucked-up family made up of drunks, bullies, and rapists.*

When Evi came in Claire was laughing hysterically repeating, "Lions, tigers and bears, oh my." Claire shared her revelation with Evi and swore that she would not follow them down that same drunken path. Evi knew how hard it was to move off of a familiar path, but she would be here when Claire was ready.

For the rest of Saturday, as the hospital staff popped in and out to perform a multitude of tests, Claire tried to sleep, moving between nightmares of her uncle and Junior. Jeremy stopped by when he could and sat quietly with Claire.

On Sunday morning, the doctor stopped by with the good news that there was no internal bleeding and Claire could go home.

Chapter Twenty-Seven

Evi helped Claire to dress in a pair of sweats and they took a cab home. Each was quiet as they reflected on the recent events: a rape, car crash, death. It was all too familiar. When they returned home, Evi put on a pot of water, searching the cabinets for some chamomile tea.

Out of the corner of her eye, Evi saw Claire take a long swing of vodka and return the bottle to its hiding place in the freezer. Evi so wanted to shake Claire and tell her that wasn't going to help, but she knew better.

They sat down with their tea, and Claire started, "Evi, I am so glad that you are here and so sorry you got pulled into this. It feels like déjà vu all over again. I am not sure why this happened or keeps happening." She broke off in uncontrollable sobs.

Evi moved closer and held her, just letting Claire get it out. She knew now was the time to tell her about her leg. She wasn't sure why this was the right time, but she knew that someone else's tragedy can often be a distraction and sometimes put things into perspective.

When Claire gained a little composure, Evi said, "We will get through this together. We will get through it all together."

That peaked Claire's attention, "All?"

"Yes," Evi said. "There is something I need to tell you, show you."

Slowly, Evi lifted her pant leg, higher and higher above the knee. Or, what was her knee.

Claire gasped—loudly—unable to control her reaction. "Oh my God, Evi, what happened?"

The two of them hugged again and cried for all that was lost.

"The war," Evi choked out, "third tour in Afghanistan. I guess third time is the charm," She joked. Evi loved to make people laugh to distract from the pain of her own life. They both laughed a little.

"I ran over an IED—sorry, an improvised explosive device—as I was running from the helicopter to collect downed soldiers in the field. As a medic, you think you are immune to the war since we are there to help and heal."

Evi continued, "About three years ago. I know I should have reached out and let you know what happened. I'm sorry, but I couldn't tell you until now. It took that long for rehab and to really learn to use this thing, my new leg. Physically, I am managing. Mentally—well that is another story for another day."

Claire looked at Evi and burst out laughing, "Well look at us, aren't we just the pair? Before she could help herself, Evi joined in until they both almost peed in their pants.

When they finally regained themselves, Evi said solemnly, "I don't want to be a victim anymore. I am ready to be a survivor, how about you?"

Claire had a pensive look on her face, and said, "Yea, me too."

With that they decided to watch movies, eat popcorn and relax for the rest of the day. They hunkered down on the couch with the cat between them, purring, Evi sipping her tea and Claire sneaking off to the freezer for some courage.

***

At some point late in the afternoon Claire's cell phone rang. It was Jeremy. *Oh Shit*, Claire thought remembering that she saw him talking to her doctor about the baby.

"Hi," she said tentatively.

"How are you?" He said concerned.

"I'm okay. Evi is here with me and we are chilling watching some movies, catching up, and resting."

"Claire," He started, but hesitated, "Dr. Ashbury told me about the baby."

Her breath caught, she did not want to think about it, talk about it, or lie about it.

"I just took the test and didn't have a chance to tell you about it."

"I'm sorry, very sorry," he said in a gravelly voice.

"Me too,"

She really wasn't sure how she felt about it. She was sorry that he thought there could have been a baby that was his. That he would grieve for a possible lie.

But she just said, "Jeremy, I love you, but I'm tired now and want to rest." Call me later with your schedule so we can have dinner this week." And, she hung up.

***

Evi waited a minute, and then cautiously offered, "Do you want to talk about it, any of it, the baby?"

"Not now, but thanks," Claire said softly, tears streaking her pale face.

Both Evi and Claire decided it was best to go to work on Monday so they began to wind down for the evening.

Claire was going to tell work that she was in a bad car accident to stave off any questions about the bruises, but realized that the attack would probably be in the paper and she was so tired of lying.

Chapter Twenty-Eight

As Claire walked into work, she realized just how sore she actually was—all over. She wanted to see June as soon as possible in case she couldn't work through the whole day.

But she was determined to stay. She wanted the distraction since she wasn't ready to think about the events of the past weekend. She grabbed a cup of coffee. *I don't need to worry about the caffeine now* she thought bitterly and headed to talk to her boss.

"Good morning June," Claire said as she hung in the doorway.

"Hey Claire, come in."

As Claire got closer, June noticed her stiff gate and with genuine concern asked, "Claire, are you ok? Please, come and sit down."

"Actually," Claire started with a nervous laugh, "Not really. I was the victim of a crime Friday night and got pretty beat up." She was reluctant to use the "R" word right now. People looked at you differently.

"Oh my gosh, was that you? I read about that in the paper. I am so sorry. Please let me know if there is anything we can do to help."

Claire said, "Thanks, my biggest concern is working full days this week. I am hoping to," she hesitated, "to keep the development of the show moving forward."

With a soft smile, June said, "Just let me know if you need any time off. I reviewed the schedule, and we are on track."

Claire had never seen this side of June and hoped it was here to stay.

"Claire, before we talk about the show, I wanted to apologize for my curt behavior during the past few weeks. I realized I was abrupt in my demands and hope to work in a closer partnership with you as a leader verses a manager."

"Funny," June continued, "I took a course last week and realized that the old style of management was out the window. That leading your resources—you and the other curators—toward agreed upon results achieves more for business and employee morale. It seems like it was a great time for that course.

With that said, I wanted to discuss with you a partnership that NMWA is forming with The Foundation for Art and Healing for your show."

"My show," Claire said softly, not sure she had even spoken that out loud.

At first Claire felt the anger rise, but from where and why she was not sure. Then, she decided to listen and learn, saying, "That sounds great."

June continued, "The Foundation for Art and Healing is very interested in working with us to offer Creative Expression Workshops to compliment the show. The public relations (PR) and marketing departments will be working with them to schedule the workshops and include the information with our marketing package for the show.

What I would like you to do is be available to support them during the workshops and participate in a practice run. I think it will give you close up and personal experience with how art can help to heal in order to support your show."

"Plus," June took a breath. "It might be just what you need in light of what you went through, are going through from the evil committed against you this weekend. I hope I didn't speak out of turn," June continued as she got a faraway look in her eyes and barely whispered, "I have been there too."

What Claire saw in June's eyes was a sadness that only another rape victim could understand. But just as quickly the steely, professional June was back.

Claire said, "Ok, that sounds exciting. Please let me know our next steps."

"Great!" June said, "The volunteers from The Foundation will be here next week for our kick off meeting. I will keep you posted on the date and time.

Chapter Twenty-Nine

With that taken care of, Claire headed to her gallery. *Her gallery*, she laughed to herself feeling a new sense of ownership.

Claire was surprised to find only two collages in the "Leaf Me Alone" series. Each was painted energetically with a blue background on a stretched canvas; creating a different experience. On one, the artist painted dark green squares over the blue background that pulled the viewer into the painting, while the other had a layer of yellow painted squares which pushed the viewer back. Each piece held four large leaves woven onto the painted background in the four-leaf clover formation, secured in the center with a large rusty piece of hardware. The leaves were sewn carefully to the canvas with thick, dark, red wool and looked as if they were being patched up from an injury.

Dear Diary...I am raw as I begin this next series. I feel naked and alone as I find myself flashing back to the hard floor I found myself on after the rape. I hear myself say my rape. I am tired of being a victim; tired of needing the bottle every time I flashback. I need to move through this. I will move through this. I hope creating two pieces will suffice this time, but only time will tell.

Still fascinated with collecting large intact fall leaves, I found eight leaves outside a meeting that I want to use here. I take deep blue paint and attack the two canvases I have laid out on my studio floor. Like Jackson Pollock, I release the paint from the brush onto the canvas with no direction, only a goal of covering both canvases. Like the paint, I feel blue, depressed, but as the paint covers the canvases, my fog starts to lift.

Yellow, I need some yellow. Where is the yellow? I start to feel panicky, needing to add some sunlight. Finding it, I feel my shoulders begin to relax. I need some structure and begin to paint squares, one inside the other. Now I need dark green, I love dark forest green, for no other reason than it reminds me of nature and growth. I repeat the pattern of squares within themselves on the other canvas. Satisfied with my foundations and feeling the grief drain out of me, I prepare the leaves with acrylic gel layers to protect them.

I feel the need to sew. I haven't sewn in a long time, but today I feel the need to sew things together, maybe to fix myself, to sew myself back together. Once the leaves are ready I start to sew four to a canvas. I sew slowly, creating long stitches, haphazardly placing them to hold each leaf down, to hold me down, to provide security.

The title hits me hard, "Leaf Me Alone." It made me laugh and cry at the same time. I am not a crier since no one needs to see how vulnerable I am. Being early in my recovery I am still struggling my way out of isolation, but not quite there yet. I crave the connection, but I don't want anyone close enough to hurt me. I finished each canvas with a large rusty piece of hardware which is my signature. Like the hardware left to weather, I too will get rusty if I am not careful...

When Claire stepped back and looked at these two pieces now hanging on the wall she felt an overwhelming push-me-pull-me sensation, not knowing which direction to go or take. After reading the related diary entry, she was amazed at how similar she was to the artist. She reflected on the rape; her rape. Not the artist's but hers. She had to sit down; not only from her physical pain, but also from the emotional burden she was carrying.

She shut and locked the gallery doors and sat. Right now she felt her rage circling in and around her, again feeling the overpowering need for a drink. *Not now*—she silently screamed, *but maybe later.*

Where did he come from? Why was Junior there at that bar? Dead! He is dead, she thought *and I'm glad. How sick was that, glad that he was dead? Glad that his dad was dead.*

Claire realized that the apple didn't fall far from the tree. She remembered her uncle dying in a car crash when she was little and how the touching then stopped.

—His death made Claire feel giddy. Everyone at her uncle's funeral was sad and crying and she had to work hard not to smile or laugh. Luckily Evi and Aunt Jo were with her, each on one side of her like pillars, holding her up, holding her hands. Evi knew how she felt and held her hand tight to help her not to laugh out loud, so tight it almost hurt—

Claire would not be attending Junior's funeral. Her mother had just called to tell her the news; she pretended to care, but said she had a big meeting at work she couldn't miss. Claire knew how her mother would react if she told her the truth behind Junior's death.

—Back in her childhood home, Claire was begging her mom to listen. "Mommy, I am not lying, he touches me in private

places when you and daddy are not around. Pleeaase make him stop." Her father once walked in on one of these pleadings and slapped her hard across the face, telling her to stop telling lies. Her mother did nothing. Nothing!—

Feeling the sharp slap of abandonment, she came back to the gallery. Was she a monster for wanting to celebrate his death, glad that Junior couldn't hurt her or any other girls? Returning her thoughts to the paintings, Claire began again to feel the push-me-pull-me sensation—glad for Junior's death, but uncertain about her feelings toward losing the baby. The rape took away her choice, her decision.

So confused, yet so relieved. How does one person feel so many things at one time? It was the feelings she didn't, couldn't deal with, the reason for a drink. *Stop It!* She screamed again to herself.

At that moment, she caught a word in the open diary— victim. It was the same thing that Evi said. She was tired of being a victim. Claire wanted to know if she had been living as a victim all these years, trying to chase away that victim with a bottle and men. *No!* She thought she just liked to party. Didn't she? What was wrong with that?

But when you party you have fun, right? When was the last time I really had fun? Claire couldn't remember since she couldn't get off the merry-go-round, going around and around with the men and booze like they were the animals on a ride. She realized she was going nowhere, actually spinning down into a dark hole all by herself.

All of a sudden the title, "Leaf Me Alone," appalled her. She now wanted to know how not to be alone, to not be a victim, how to heal.

Funny, how Evi was back in her life at this exact moment, and how she was given this collection and show to curate. She wasn't sure she believed in fate, but maybe there was something watching over her after all.

Chapter Thirty

Claire moved through the next couple of days in a fog. She felt anxious and fearful most of the time. But for any on-looker, she was the picture of perfection. Her hair was always washed and neat, her outfit crisp, and her smile infectious; a mask she wore to the outside world to say she was "fine."

As her body healed, her mind took on a life of its own; spinning, constantly spinning. Feeling herself pulled back into the alley, being raped again and again, wondering why and what had she done wrong. *Why was Junior there?* Feeling her head smash against the cement wall as his fists pounded her flesh and he tore into her.

How could anyone, especially family, do this? Sometimes her thoughts took her to her childhood bedroom when her uncle Bob was babysitting and the touching would begin again, then back to the alley, and again to her childhood bedroom. Around and around her mind went, cycling her into fear and darkness.

Claire waded her way through the thick, dark days until, after work; she could escape into a local bar. When she got home—slightly drunk—she joked to Evi that, per WTOP, a glass of wine a day was like "an apple a day to keep the doctor away."

***

But Evi knew better. Claire's proclamation was only an out loud agreement giving her permission for that first glass of wine, which always turned into more.

Evi knew only too well that one was too many and a thousand never enough. *Never enough* Evi repeated to herself, remembering the hole she tried to drink herself out of. Closing that mental door, she turned her thoughts to helping Claire. But when Evi tried to engage Claire to share her experience, Claire changed the subject.

The only thing Claire wanted to talk about was Jeremy, the engagement, and upcoming wedding, which had no date. It all seemed like a fantasy to Evi, someone that Claire found safety in, could hide in. In the early stages after a severe trauma, Evi knew this could seem helpful in the healing process, but it was really just a form of denial that could backfire when the fantasy popped and reality set in.

***

The night Jeremy finally called, Claire was agitated. "Why did it take him so long to call?" she snapped out loud, "Doesn't he know that I need him?"

"Hey Babe," he said when Claire answered the phone.

Babe? She hated that term. It reminded her of those long ago dark days with her uncle. *Why didn't Jeremy know that?*

—*"Come on Babe, no one will know. You know I love you and this doesn't hurt,"* Uncle Bob said in a syrupy, sweet voice, *"But if you do tell someone, you will get hurt Babe."* His voice turning mean and commanding, *"Understand? And, you don't want me to hurt you or anyone else in your family, do you?"*

"No," She whimpered softly.

His voice turned sweet again, continuing to touch her as he said "That's my good girl, my Babe."—

Claire came back to the present when she heard Jeremy ask, "Claire, are you there?"

Claire said, "Hi, yes, I'm here," holding onto tears so tight her face hurt.

***

"How are you?" Jeremy pursued gently, for he was a healer but didn't know anything about this type of injury. He had talked to Dr. Ashbury to understand what he could expect and was surprised to learn that recovery from rape, especially a violent rape like this one, was complicated and could take years. *Years!* Jeremy knew he had little patience which is why he chose the ER for his residency. His patients were not chronic. They had episodic injuries or issues that he could stitch up or perform quick general surgery on and send them on their way. He loved the uncertainty of the ER, not knowing what each day would bring, never getting bored, feeding off the immediate rush and excitement.

Claire replied softly, "Fine, I'm just fine."

One of Jeremy's college girlfriends used to joke that "fine" meant fucked up, insane, neurotic, and excitable. He realized that today, it wasn't funny. It was going to be a long ride for Claire, one he couldn't take. And, he wondered how he could end the engagement; bow out gracefully, without any more damage to Claire.

"Good," He said, "I'm glad. I'm booked in the ER for the next week so how about I call you next week for dinner."

"That sounds good, talk to you later," Claire said.

***

Claire was relieved and sad all at once, fixing it with a swig of vodka. She wondered how long she had been standing in the open freezer and giggling to herself wondering what WTOP would say about a swig of vodka a day.

Claire absently said goodnight to Evi. As she cried herself to sleep, Claire contemplated how she should end the engagement.

Chapter Thirty-One

When Claire got to work on Thursday, she reviewed two pieces that took a softer, more subtle approach from the previous artwork. The artist continued to use found objects from nature, but this time added a layer of rice paper to hide and expose these elements.

The one entitled, "Out of the Dark," only showed small areas of light as it revealed the hidden treasures below the black paper.

Dear Diary...Today I am feeling the pull into the darkness, but didn't want to go there. I am tired of living in the problem; tired of experiencing it over and over again. So I went through my collection of dried flowers and sticks and glued them to two canvases. I laid black rice paper over one of the canvases and brushed on a lot of acrylic gel. I love how the paper took on the shape of the dried flowers and sticks, creating a three-dimensional texture. In places, I tore the paper away to show light poking through the darkness since I do not want to live in the darkness anymore...

Despite her best intentions, Claire was drawn into this piece. It was dark and foreboding, yet light at the same time, like there was hope. But the dark was more imposing than the light was refreshing, keeping her drawn to the darkness.

Claire called Herb, who carefully hung "Out of the Dark" and its companion piece entitled "Out From Under the Snow." This one is brighter, cleaner, with the treasures clear under the white paper, yet still apparently hidden.

Dear Diary...I continued to experiment with the rice paper. "Out from Under the Snow" is inspired by the raging snow storm outside and what the ground and its treasures will look like as the snow starts to melt allowing them to show through to their true natures, to claim their own value.

What is my value? And, why does my artwork always kick me in my ass? Dammit - answer me! Why is my value tied up in my tragedy? I am tired of being my tragedy, I am ready to move on and claim my value for who I am, not what has happened to me...

Claire liked this piece; it reminded her of how spring was peeking right around the corner as snow melted. It reminded her of playing in Aunt Jo's yard and feeling the crunch of life waiting to spring forward from the snow. But reading the artist's diary gave Claire pause, as she wondered whether her value was tied up in her tragedies. Or was she living her life running from her tragedies? Trying to find safety from them, hiding in plain site within the bottle?

This piece and corresponding diary entry were kicking her ass. *How much did I drink this week anyway?* Thinking about her recycle bin littered with wine bottles, there were really too many to count. Funny, but she didn't remember Evi drinking since she came to live with her. And, they used to knock back some strong ones, competing for who could stay on their stools by the end of the night.

Why wasn't Evi drinking? She had lost a leg for God's sake. That would make me drink. I had been raped and beaten, don't I deserve to drink? But does that keep me in the rape, circling over and over on that merry-go-round just trading one horse for another?

Claire realized that she wanted the noise in her head to stop. She wondered how she could walk through the rape, straight through the rape to the other side. She could see the artist healing through her artwork, as painful as that might be and was actually looking forward to the partnership with the Foundation for Art and Healing.

Chapter Thirty-Two

On Friday morning, Claire was very surprised when she unpacked the piece entitled "Patterns" since it was totally different from any of the other pieces in this collection. It was impersonal as the artist used mostly manmade materials. It appeared to be a construction, deconstruction, and reconstruction allowing the artist to proceed to a different place from where she started. When Claire inadvertently turned the piece over she was surprised to find the following written on the back.

"Patterns bubbled up like they just went around and around with nowhere to go. Patterns, like the unmanageability of my life."

Claire was intrigued and mystified as she reached for the artist's diary.

Dear Diary...I almost threw out this piece when I was cleaning up my studio; thinking it wasn't important. But it is actually very important and relevant to my life helping me to recognize that to move away from destructive patterns will take self-construction and growth.

I started with a large piece of foam core and created a collage by gluing a variety of bright rice papers in an abstract arrangement with a mixture of glossy and mat acrylic gel medium. I love these thick rice papers. I discovered them at Crunchies, a natural pet food store in Crofton, Maryland. They were a fund raiser for police dogs to buy protective gear for them. The rice papers came in beautiful bright colors with textures from their natural materials.

Once the collage dried, I had this intense urge to randomly cut the entire piece into shapes. So I took out my surgical knife and went to work, being careful not to slice off a finger. Then I wanted to secure the pieces with shiny new hardware. So this took me on a hunt to the hardware store for specific nuts and bolts. I love those adventures for they take me out of myself, helping me to fully engage in the creative process.

I then rearranged and screwed the pieces back together into a new whole piece of art. Kinda like screwing my life back together. This piece was exhausting. In the past, I was on the hunt for another person or thing to take me out of myself. This piece was a true expression of where I was and didn't want to be anymore—insane. I remember reading that repeating the same thing over and over and expecting different results is insanity. You would think that a productive working girl wouldn't be insane. But this piece proves otherwise. Now that I am aware of and can see these patterns I can face the parts of me I don't like and slowly start to change them, creating new patterns...

Claire was thunderstruck by the time she put down the diary. *Wow!* What type of patterns had she developed from her past, her father's and mother's pasts, that have encroached themselves in her life?

For some reason, she thought about luggage. It seemed to her that everyone came into life with a set of luggage. Her father's was probably black and hard-edged; her mom's pink, soft, and falling apart. A marriage should be a merging of luggage, everyone discarding ones that do not match anymore and eventually ending up with a set that matched and happily worked together. Then this new luggage should be handed down to the kids to use, improve and pass on. But what if the luggage was never upgraded, never merged, and instead just thrown at the children as is?

Luggage seemed like patterns to her, continually being used over and over again. She thought about the last few weekends before the rape and how she went out drinking and left with a different man. *Am I insane, repeating the same thing over and over again, expecting different results? Was this my pattern, my set of luggage? What am I looking for: intimacy, sex, excitement, control, love?*

Her mind lingered angrily on the word "love." *What about love? What was love anyway? A drunken daddy who always screamed at the family and hit me when he could catch me? An uncle and cousin who sexually abused and raped me? A mommy more interested in staying out of the way, than in protecting me, her child?*

Claire thought *and what about the drinking?*

"Whose drinking?" a voice in her head said, "Yours or your father's?"

Now where did that come from and what was wrong with my drinking? She managed at work, even excelled, picking up the Art and Healing collection to curate on her own. She was nothing like her father. That piece of luggage definitely did not get passed down to her. *Or did it?* Did that that black with pink flowered luggage really get passed down to her?

She was feeling tired all of a sudden. Dead down, draggy tired so she headed to the staff lounge to get a coke.

Passing by the great hall, Claire smelled it before she saw it— the left over tray of cocktails from the mid-morning wedding. Her heart raced excitedly at the thought of sneaking one of those drinks. She drank down half of her soda to make room.

She suddenly felt like throwing up. How could she feel repulsed by her behavior, on the one hand, and seek it at the same time? What was wrong with her, what type of patterns did she get cursed with? Was it in her blood to drink? Was she really a party girl or did she have to drink?

All she knew was that she still wanted a drink to make it all stop. With that she took a half empty glass off the tray. She went into the bathroom and quickly poured it into her coke. She curled her lips around that can and finished her drink. She headed home determined to throw away all of her black with pink flowered luggage.

Chapter Thirty-Three

Claire called Evi on the way home to see what they should have for dinner. They settled on Indian food which Claire picked up. While preparing the table for dinner, they chatted about their day, and Claire had a glass of wine.

A couple times, Claire thought she saw the black with pink flowered luggage stubbornly refusing to leave her closet.

Really Claire thought, saying "I am in control here. If I say go, you will go!"

The luggage laughed at her and said, "I don't think so, we are here to stay."

Confused, Evi said, "Are you talking to me?"

With that Claire got a glass out of the cabinet and filled it with the frozen vodka, saying, "I'll show you who is boss."

But then the glass slipped from her hand, falling to the floor, shattering. Claire sank down and started to cry, trying to put the glass back together, trying to stop the vodka from getting away, and screaming as she cut her hands.

***

Evi stood by watching her, blood dripping from Claire's wounds. Evi was waiting for the opportunity to help, waiting for Claire's gift of desperation.

Then Evi heard it. Claire crying uncontrollably sobbing, screaming, "I can't do this anymore, I need help. Can you please help me; I feel so lost and out of control." Miraculously the black and pink flowered luggage went away and Claire only saw a light in Evi's eyes where she knew she would find hope.

Evi gently removed Claire from the mess in the kitchen and bandaged her hands; glad again that she had become a medic, a healer. They sat on the couch and Evi let her cry, holding her like a baby, repeating over and over, "I know, I know, it will be okay, I promise you."

Claire continued to babble like a baby about not being able to stop, not sure if she could stop drinking, wasn't sure how to, feeling confident one minute and crazy the next. Evi continued to rock her, promising to stay with her, but she said that there was someplace they needed to go, and helped Claire get dressed.

Claire whined, "Why do we need to go out, I'm tired and don't want to go anywhere."

Evi sensed her fear, remembering only too well her own and told Claire that where they were going, she would be safe. It was a warm night and Claire let Evi guide her to the taxi and then into the church.

"Why are we going into a church?" Claire whined some more.

Evi answered, "We are meeting some friends for a big celebration."

Claire was not happy about any type of celebration when she felt that her life was ending, but she went along.

The room was large and chairs were set out in rows. There was coffee brewing in the back and a large cake that said *Congratulations—Two years!* At the front, there was a table with two chairs. Evi got a cup of coffee for both of them and set Claire down in the front row.

A couple of Evi's friends sat on both sides of Claire to provide pillars of support. Evi had texted them on the way in that she needed help with a newcomer and they were ready. One of them was Mercy, a skinny, tallish woman in her late forties. She had skin the texture of leather, eyes as hard as granite, and salt and peppered hair all of which were set off by her bright, contagious smile.

Evi took her place in the other seat at the front table and her male companion started the meeting with the serenity prayer:

God grant me the serenity to accept the things I cannot change, the courage to change the things I can and the wisdom to know the difference.

The man then said, "This is a special night and a wonderful evening for a celebration. With that, I will turn it over to Evi.

"Hi, I'm Evi and I am an alcoholic. Welcome to my old and new friends that have found their way here today. Today is my two year anniversary. I have been clean and sober and not touched a drink for the past two years."

Claire sat there with her nostrils flaring and her arms folded tightly a crossed her chest. *How could Evi drag me here? I am not an alcoholic!* But then tears started to slide down Claire's face for she also lived the story she now heard.

Evi's abandonment—her mother died of a drug overdose, her father went to jail. How Claire brought Evi, disheveled and sad, home from elementary school for Aunt Jo to take care of and adopt. How Aunt Jo fought hard against the system to keep and adopt Evi. How Evi and Claire used drugs and alcohol throughout high school.

The rest of the story was new to Claire and she listened intently, wanting to know what happened to her best and oldest friend. Evi continued with how the drinking had turned into something destructive once she joined the army and became a medic. In Afghanistan Evi realized that she couldn't save everyone; which is why she became a medic. Soldiers, men and women, came to her in all states, blown to hell, missing arms and legs, or if whole in body, missing pieces of their soul and brain that they left on the battlefield.

So she bandaged them up the best she could and sent them on their way to military hospitals, not knowing if they made it or not, not knowing if she saved them. The bottle was her savior; it helped her make it all go away. She felt like she was just one of the guys, letting off steam. Then it happened. She was running to get some wounded and stepped on an IED and lost her own leg. She was now the wounded and needed a medic.

She survived and ended up back in the states three years ago and started physical recovery. But her mental recovery was slow to catch up and the bottle became her best friend.

It was through an angel at rehab, who had also lost a limb and saw where Evi was going, that helped to steer Evi to real recovery. She basically told Evi that she had two choices: one— end up on the street an active alcoholic alone, begging for money, and living in the problem; or two—accept her situation and get into the solution to rejoin life and become a real healer.

At that point, Evi realized that she had been given her gift of desperation and put the bottle down.

Evi learned that until you are sick and tired of being sick and tired that you will not be able to put down the bottle and accept the solution—the twelve steps of recovery.

Claire almost gasped out loud. That was it! She was sick and tired of being sick and tired. She found her gift of desperation on that kitchen floor a couple of hours ago. Looking down at her bandaged hands, she almost hoped the cuts would leave scars to always remind her.

She also realized that if Evi could not drink for two years after everything she had been through, that she could do it too.

At that moment, she heard Evi say, "I learned that just for today, I don't have to drink. And, that is what I have been doing, one day at a time, not drinking and working this 12 step program. Today I face my fears, doubts, and insecurities instead of drinking them away."

The meeting was closed and the group got up and formed a circle around the perimeter of the room. Everyone held hands and they said a couple more prayers to close the meeting.

Claire looked around and was awestruck to see how many people made up the circle. While she felt scared, she also felt hope for the first time in a long time. She had a hard time getting close to Evi as everyone was hugging and congratulating her.

The lady next to her kept a tight hold of her hand and introduced herself, "Hi, my name is Mercy and Evi tells me that you need a sponsor. I would be honored if you will let me help you."

"Sure," Claire said, "but I don't know what that means, or what we do."

Mercy exchanged numbers with Claire and told Claire to call her early tomorrow to plan her day.

"Plan my day?" Claire said.

"Yes," said Mercy, "tomorrow will be the first day you won't drink; it can be a hard day, so we need a plan. Can you make a commitment that you won't drink tonight?"

"I think so," Claire said tentatively, and then more clearly, "Yes, I will."

Mercy said, "Good," and slowly let go of her hand. "Talk to you tomorrow and have a grateful night."

Claire said good night as Evi finally made her way over to her. She wondered what a grateful night meant and was glad Evi was going home with her—their home.

Evi gave her a big hug and said, "Welcome to AA Sis, we've been waiting for you."

Chapter Thirty-Four

When they got home Claire automatically went for the freezer to retrieve her vodka until she saw the bloody towels on the counter and the broken glass in the sink.

She sank down and screamed, "What is wrong with me? I just promised Mercy I wouldn't drink tonight and the first thing I do is reach for the vodka."

Looking down at her bandaged hands, she started to cry hysterically.

Evi made them both a cup of chamomile tea and helped Claire to the couch. Claire accepted the tea and started to relax.

Evi finally said, "Two years ago, I was ready to give up. I had drunk myself into a stupor and could hardly stand up enough to balance in order to use my new leg. I too found myself on the floor screaming in pain, from my phantom leg and the alcohol drowning my brain. I later learned that my leg hurt more because of the drinking.

I thought I could control my drinking, but the more I tried, the harder it was and the more I drank. I barely remember the first few days after I decided I needed help and couldn't manage it on my own. But I made it through. I am not going to lie to you, this is going to be a rough weekend as you detox from alcohol. It is painful but necessary. But, you won't be alone—I will be with you the whole time."

Claire curled herself into Evi and cried herself to sleep.

***

When Claire woke up, she hurt all over. Her hands burned and she wondered what the bandages were from. Her body hurt from the rape and she had a splitting headache; a hangover unequal to any she had experienced before. She wasn't sure how she got into her bed and gasped when she found Evi sleeping next to her.

Evi stirred and said, "Good morning, Sunshine. No, we didn't sleep together, if that is what's got your worried. You're not my type anyway." Evi let out a little snort, and continued,

"Now let's get you some water and Tylenol for that headache and some food in your belly."

Claire grumbled back, "Ok," thinking how did Evi know? And, food was the last think she wanted right now.

It was slowly coming back to her, the broken glass of vodka, how she cut up her hands, the AA meeting—her promise not to drink. Who was she supposed to call?

"I am supposed to call someone called a sponsor," She slurred to Evi. Claire picked up her jeans off the floor, almost falling on her face, and found a slip of paper in her back pocket. "Mercy, I am supposed to call someone named Mercy. What kind of name is that anyway?" Claire sputtered.

"A sponsor is someone who guides you through the twelve steps of the AA program," Evi answered, "You will give her a call after you eat."

Claire thought stubbornly, *Will I now?*

But Claire did. Mercy answered on the second ring and was happy to hear from her.

"Do you remember any of our conversation from last night?"

"Not really," Claire said.

"The most important thing," Mercy said, "is that you don't pick up a drink today. I know it is going to be hard and you are going to feel like shit as the alcohol leaves your system, but each day will get better. Kinda like a real bad case of the flu. Also, I want you to go to ninety meetings in ninety days."

Who does she think she is? Claire thought, *bossing me around like this.* She retaliated, "I am very busy and that won't work."

Mercy had heard it all before, herself included. She knew that no one at this stage has anything like a clear thought. So she didn't budge. "If you really want help, then you will go to ninety meetings in ninety days. Either Evi or I will go with you."

"What is this, the *Sisterhood of the Traveling Pants*?" Claire shot back.

Mercy laughed, "Yep, something like that. See you tonight."

Tonight seemed like a long time away and all Claire wanted to do was sleep, which Evi let her do until lunch.

At lunch time, Evi gently woke Claire, fed her, forced her to drink juice and take more Tylenol. She then put Claire back to bed. Evi repeated the same thing for dinner. But this time, she told Claire to take a shower and get dressed that it was time for a meeting.

Claire was feeling a little better, but not much. She barely remembered her talk this morning with someone named Mercy and that she needed to go to a meeting. Good thing, since what she really wanted to do was get a drink and find someone to fuck really hard—*God I'm a mess.*

***

Claire and Evi headed out to the meeting to meet Mercy. Claire was pleasantly surprised that she enjoyed the meeting and related to the stories she heard. Mercy encouraged her to pick up a white chip for twenty-four hours. *I did it,* she realized! She had not had a drink today and was very proud of her chip. She noticed a guy watching her and felt that familiar pull.

As she turned to pounce, Mercy grabbed her hand and said, "Let's talk."

"Not now," Claire said forcefully, "I'll be right back."

Before Claire could gain any ground, Mercy spun her around, looking her squarely in her face, and said, "I understand. I too used booze and men to fill that empty place. Now that the booze is gone, the need for men will feel uncontrollable. But for me to get better, really better, I needed to abstain from both—just for today.

So, you need to ask yourself, what do you really want? Another hollow night with someone you don't know and doesn't really care about you, or a chance to get better? If you are not sure, think about the events of the past couple weeks and let me know if you still want to keep repeating that insanity over and over again."

Claire burst into tears. "Wh.. wh.. why am I like this? What is wrong with me?"

Mercy held her tight and said, "You are okay now and we will figure all that out together."

Evi took Claire home and they repeated the same thing the next day, creating new patterns.

Chapter Thirty-Five

By Monday morning, Claire wasn't sure she felt strong enough to go to work. She still heard a woodpecker pounding between her ears. Her heart felt heavy and her mind would not stop spinning. Mercy, who stopped by for coffee, and Evi convinced Claire that work was the best thing for her.

Mercy added, "Use the phone, we are only a phone call away."

She was told to go in and focus on her job and to do the best she could since that is what they pay her to do.

Evi explained, "I went right back to work. By focusing on helping other wounded warriors, I got out of myself and felt better.

Out of myself, Claire thought giggling to herself, *now there's a concept.*

She was also instructed to come right home after work, eat dinner, and get ready for a meeting.

"Yes, mothers!" Claire snapped indignantly.

***

As she headed for work, she passed the Irish bar and felt the familiar tug. It wasn't opened yet, so there was safety in that, but she knew that tonight would be different. She remembered Mercy talking about having a plan and sticking to it. Claire also told herself that just for today she didn't have to drink or fuck and that she wasn't alone.

When Claire entered the NMWA, she remembered the book, *Are You There God? It's Me, Margaret,* by Judy Blume; and thought, *God, it's me Claire. If you can hear me, please help me today.*

Before heading to the gallery, Claire took a moment to stop by the Renaissance section to view the Madonna and Child portrait to get grounded.

Before she was ready to go to the Gallery June caught up with her and said, "Good morning Claire, how are you feeling?"

"Thanks for asking, I'm getting better," feeling that familiar anxiety creep in.

"I am glad I caught you. First, the write-ups for the *Art and Healing* exhibit are very good. Keep up the good work and let Shelby also know."

Claire's anxiety started to slip away.

"Second, before you start working on the exhibit, the Foundation for Art and Healing folks will be here this morning. We will meet with them in half an hour to discuss the Creative Expression Workshops they will be conducting with you. See you in my conference room shortly."

"Ok," Claire replied, sounding more confident than she felt.

She had forgotten about the workshops and started to panic. Instead of relaxing into the Madonna and Child portrait, her eyes wandered to the Fruit and Wine still life a few pieces away. The empty glass in the painting seemed to magically fill up with wine and float out to her. She found her hand reaching out to take it.

Wow! I am a crazy bitch Claire thought, quickly putting her hand into her purse to look for her phone. With only a couple minutes to spare, she called Mercy to tell her what happened.

Mercy laughed which broke the tension and said, "Floating wine glasses, now that is a new one." Her voice grew serious, "Claire, stay away from that painting and focus on the kick-off meeting today. See you at the meeting tonight."

Claire felt herself relax and the overpowering need for a drink faded like a sunset. This was just a kick-off meeting to learn about the Creative Expression Workshops and their schedule in relation to the exhibit. Claire allowed herself to want to learn something new and see how her role played out.

***

Claire entered June's conference room and met the partners from the Foundation. There were three of them, the Director, the Coordinator, Ben and his Assistant, Cora. The Director was there to give an overview of the Foundation's work and kick-off the partnership with the NMWA. Claire would be working directly with Ben and Cora. Ben had light, olive skin, jet black hair, and deep blue eyes that looked like they had seen too much. He was about 5'10" and had a strong medium build.

Cora was very short, a little heavy with caramel colored skin and warm brown eyes. Claire immediately felt comfortable with both of them. They were interested in the exhibit and wanted to see the progress if that was possible. Claire said it was about seventy-five percent done and she would be happy to walk them all through it.

They discussed the three workshops they would facilitate: a free cutting collage, related writing exercise, and mask painting. They wanted to do each set of workshops with teens and adults who had been through traumatic experiences. Claire thought *I definitely qualify for "traumatic experiences."*

There were also representatives from the NMWA marketing and PR departments who would handle the scheduling, publicity, and registration. The Director suggested that the NMWA team do the exercises also as a good premise for marketing them and supporting the actual public workshops.

June agreed but said, "I'm concerned about getting my entire team together at one time due to already set schedules."

The Director said they could run a mini version of each workshop. June agreed and asked the PR rep to set a morning and afternoon session for Wednesday, Thursday, and Friday of this week.

They then all agreed that the public workshops would coincide with the opening of the exhibit.

***

Claire took the Foundation group to the gallery to see the exhibit in progress. Some of the updated descriptions were up and they were impressed. They wanted to know if Claire knew who the artist was.

"No," Claire said honestly, "the exhibit was donated from an anonymous estate and we don't even have the artist's name. But due to the artwork and diaries we are able to curate the exhibit to show how the artist healed using art to work her way through her life and challenging events."

As June listened from behind the group, she was impressed with Claire's understanding of the exhibit and ability to step out of her Renaissance box.

Chapter Thirty-Six

Claire met Ben and Cora in the workshop room Wednesday afternoon and was surprised to be the only one there; finding out that everyone else had joined in the morning session. Cora began by explaining that the purpose for the exercise, for any creative exercise, is to express feelings.

"Not dealing with our feelings can keep us sick," Cora said, "locking us into anger, anxiety, and/or fear that can manifest itself into all sorts of physical illnesses, like heart attacks or ulcers."

Ben continued saying, "Guilt and shame can lead to and keep us locked into self-destructive behaviors, like drinking and addictions, for years. Basically, we are as sick as our secrets."

Cora finished with, "Feelings are not facts, but they can keep us prisoner. By expressing our feelings and understanding them, we can move through them and forward with our lives, creating healthy lives."

They definitely had Claire's attention and she wondered what type of feelings she had been harboring or hiding from.

They directed Claire to the materials in front of her: glue sticks, copy paper, scissors, and lots of magazines. There was also a big box of tissues. Ben told her that in this workshop she would create a collage. She was to think of a traumatic event and how it made her feel. She should cut or tear out pictures and words from the magazines that represented those feelings.

A collage, they explained was a random placement of images and words on to a sheet of paper to create a unified picture. She could glue them down as she cut them out or place them on the paper and rearrange them before she glued them down. She would have an hour.

Cora asked Claire if she had a traumatic event in mind.

Claire's heart raced and she started to sweat. She couldn't go back into that alley. But something told her she had to if she wanted to stop drinking.

"Okay," she whispered.

Ben put on some soft background music, the Nora Jones station on Pandora, and set the timer on his watch. There was also a Do Not Disturb sign on the door to maintain privacy. The Director had explained to June, that this was necessary to help folks in the workshops feel safe.

***

Claire sat perfectly still for what felt like hours, staring straight ahead into that dark alley. Ben and Cora, while not art therapists, were certified in these workshops. Ben sat down next to Claire feeling the fear radiating from her.

Softly he said, "Claire, you are safe here. I am right here and will not leave you alone."

Alone she thought. *Not alone—good.*

"Can you choose a magazine to start flipping through?" Ben asked gently.

Without thinking Claire grabbed the first magazine and started to flip through it until she saw a pair of eyes that she needed. She tore them out. Tearing felt good. She placed it on her copy paper. After that first tear, she was on a roll. She went through three magazines, tearing, cutting and placing, over and over until she was exhausted; her heart finally slowing down.

She stopped for a minute thinking *you son of a bitch, Junior, you don't own me anymore, and neither does your father.*

Wiping away her tears, Claire got focused, arranged her nuggets to her satisfaction and used a glue stick to lock them down. She took a sip of water and felt lighter than she had in days. In all her art schooling, she had never experienced anything like this. She was always so precise in her portraits, so confining. She was overwhelmed and excited by this freedom.

Ben gave her a folder to house her collage and told her not to look at it now. That they were going to put it away and revisit it tomorrow at the next workshop. Claire obliged.

***

Claire was done for the day and glad to be heading home and to a meeting. She called Mercy on her way out. As she walked by her favorite Irish bar, Claire told her about the day's events. Mercy said she needed to share that at the meeting.

Claire balked, sounding like a petulant child, and said "I will not!"

Mercy told Claire how she felt the same way when her sponsor told her it was time to share. How scared she was to share her stuff, but she said, "We are only as sick as our secrets. That if we want to feel better, we don't have an option but to share."

There it is again Claire thought. *I am only as sick as my secrets. I am so tired of feeling sick.* In a small voice she said, "Ok."

After dinner and some quality time with her cat, Tabitha, Claire and Evi headed off to the meeting.

Sharing was not as hard as she thought. In fact, others came up afterwards to share their experience, strength, and hope about similar situations and she started to feel like she had come home.

Chapter Thirty-Seven

The next day Claire joined the morning workshop, leery but excited to see what lay in store for today. There were a few people this time. Ben and Cora returned everyone's collages and said that today they would spend an hour writing about what they saw.

When Claire opened her folder she was surprised and shocked to see the words "You Don't Own Me" pasted on top of her pictures. The words were from different articles and fonts but very plain to see.

Her hour of writing was exhilarating. The pen danced across the page like it had a life of its own, releasing pent up fears like wild horses released from a corral.

***

Ben noticed she was glowing and he hid a secret smile, for he could see the healing power of art. When they started yesterday he didn't know if there was a tragic event in her life or if she was just participating in the work assignment. But today he could tell by her face, that something positive happened from her creative writing assignment and that whatever it was would lose its hold on her, like it did for him.

***

Cora told the group that the next step for today's workshop was to talk about their experience from the two exercises they have done to date.

Cora continued, "I know how hard it is to talk about feelings that have been buried or confusing. You don't need to share specifics, but it would be helpful for the group to share some thoughts so that they can understand what the patrons who will join these workshops might go through." Everyone took their turn and revealed what they learned from the experience.

While Claire did not disclose any details, she was able to share with her co-workers that something had been bothering her for a long time and she felt a wonderful release. She also said that she was surprised to start to understand the true healing power of art. These exercises gave her a fresh perspective on her collection and what the artist actually experienced as she released herself onto her canvases.

With that, Claire headed off to work on her show.

Chapter Thirty-Eight

Claire unwrapped "Anger" and found a very raw, hot piece. And, it did radiate anger through intense brush strokes of thick yellow, black and red paint. The red paint suggested that the artist was slashed to her core; bleeding from self-imposed wounds making this a very compelling, intense and disturbing piece.

Dear Diary...I am angry today. Really Angry! I have been around program for a while and yet I seem to forget how *cunning, baffling and powerful* this disease is. How the dragon continues to elicit fire. Why I need to be vigilant on a daily basis. Why there is no real cure for this disease, only a daily reprieve. I don't know how it happened, but it did, back to day one, picking up another twenty-four hour chip.

Black and blue from the beating I got from who knows where. Trying to outrun the insanity again, thinking I could manage it, control it. I didn't know what to do with all this anger, so before I got drunk again, I got out a blank canvas which I layered with torn up journal pages full of despair, disgust and desperation in being lost again in addiction.

Then I painted layers and layers of paint. I found some sort of clear plastic beads in my studio that I added to the red paint to give my anger substance and grit. I painted more layers of paint until I was all worn out—exhausted—having spent my anger into those furious brush strokes.

I added a timer face upside down to depict lost time! Time was moving on without me due to my anger. This is what addiction is to me. This is what unmanageability and craziness looks like. Again! How could I be here again after putting down the booze and drugs years ago and still so caught up in anger...

Claire felt drawn into this piece, its raw energy, the anger, her own rising close to the surface. But she must control it. She must never let anyone see what she is really made of, where her anger and rage can take her against those that hurt her; against those that might hurt her.

As she focused on this piece, she found herself falling back twenty years.

—Feeling his hands on her—what was he doing and why won't he stop? I am screaming, can't anyone here me screaming. Why can't I breathe? How many hands does he have? One is over my mouth, the other on my body. I am trying to scream, trying to breathe; trying to bite him to release me. Falling deeper inside myself, going to a place of nowhere until he finished—

Swimming back to the surface of now, Claire sputtered as the anger and hurt raged to the surface. She wanted to scream, but she was at work, it would have to wait. The bottle was her scream, allowing her to go back to that place of nowhereness, silencing the scream that so needed to be released. But she couldn't go to the bottle; it was not an option today.

So instead she called Mercy to tell her how she was drowning in anger and to ask for help. Mercy was there, she was always there, like an angel. Like Aunt Jo.

Mercy said that the anger was ok; actually important and just to walk through it to the other side. She explained that it would slowly go away a little each day. But if we try to control it with the booze and men that it will then find a home and grow roots.

With a small laugh, Mercy told Claire that what she does is say, "Anger, thanks for stopping by, but I don't need you today."

Claire thought that was ridiculous, but tried it and the anger miraculously receded to a low simmer. With that, Claire left for the day, walking past the Irish bar and its wine cellar.

***

That night, after the meeting, Claire said to Evi, "Let's FaceTime Aunt Jo."

Evi screamed, "Yea! I wonder where she is since she never stays in one place for long. Let's do it!"

So they started FaceTime. When Aunt Jo answered, both girls had their faces scrunched together in the little camera.

"Well hello there girls don't you look so silly! How are you doing?" cooed Aunt Jo.

After both Claire and Evi chit-chatted about their careers and said they were fine, they busted out laughing, and screeched in unison, "Where are you now?"

"Well girls hold on to your knickers! I have taken up residency at a big, beautiful farm in Florida. I've decided to grow roots here. I think I'll call it Ruby Ranch. 'Ruby' for the slippers in the *Wizard of Oz* movie, and 'Ranch' because it reminds me of a big ranch in Texas. Hope y'all will come visit soon. We are setting up a quilting shop, classrooms, and retreat center in a beautiful refurbished red barn. There will also be private studios for the artists in the family," Aunt Jo said as she winked at Claire.

Laughing, they said, "We'll be there. Luv ya lots!"

"Luv ya lots back," Aunt Jo said blowing a long stream of air kisses.

When they hung up, Claire and Evi were laughing. They both spun around and around the room, clicking their heels together three times screaming, "I want to go to Ruby Ranch. Take me to Ruby Ranch."

Chapter Thirty-Nine

Feeling refreshed on Friday morning, Claire joined the third workshop group. The tables were covered with brown paper, paints, and brushes. Plastic masks were laid out for each seat. Ben welcomed the NMWA group to the last practice workshop and proceeded to give instructions.

"The mask is you. We are going to start by painting the outside which represents you to the outside world."

Claire wasn't sure about this exercise since the outside world saw exactly who she was, sunshiny, happy, and professional. She picked up a thick paint brush and dipped it into bright yellow paint. She covered the entire mask with deliberate brush strokes, slow and steady to make sure all of the white was gone.

She changed brushes, resting the used yellow one in a cup of water, and found the orange paint. She proceeded to paint rays in orange extending out from and around the eyes, like the sun. She added a red line to each sun ray for emphasis. Claire then painted red around the open mouth to make sure it looked like a smile.

Everyone was told to clean their brushes and take a 15 minute break. When they returned, Cora instructed them to now paint the inside of the mask, explaining that this is the part we don't show to the outside world.

The sunshine faded and the anger boiled up out of nowhere. Claire instinctually reached for the black and red paint. She couldn't decide which to start with. So she dipped into the black paint and started to cover the inside of the mask. Then the red called and she added sharp shapes with quick ragged brush strokes.

She couldn't stop and wondered why. When she finally finished, the mouth looked like a hot scream with a staggering, red, lightning bolt running through the face. She was agitated and exhilarated all at once. The inside of the mask oozed anger, raw anger, almost too hot to touch.

Ben took over again and said that, after cleaning up, they would have a show and tell. Participants could choose which side to share with the group.

Claire was not ready to face the inside, so she displayed the sunny outside. Some co-workers showed their inside and it seemed to represent the same thing she experienced from them at work. *Why was mine so different? What was wrong with me?*

"Claire," she heard the vodka—that used to live in her purse—call loudly. She wondered if anyone else in the workshop had heard it. Watching Ben approach, Claire felt her coochy-coochy start to heat up. She was dizzy with anticipation.

***

Ben came over and asked her if she was ok. He had watched her internal struggle from across the room. He knew the anguish of living with Dr. Jekyll and Mr. Hyde and what the inside mask could reveal. That is why he loved to run these workshops. Once revealed, Mr. Hyde could be expressed and eliminated.

***

"I'm not sure," Claire said, glad that her co-workers and Cora had gone to lunch. "That was a pretty powerful exercise."

"Can I see the inside?" Ben asked, reaching for her mask, which Claire now held protectively in her lap.

"No!" Claire snapped. Feeling bad, she joked, "I guess so, but it's not a pretty sight."

"That's ok," Ben laughed, "I'm sure I've seen worse."

Reluctantly, she let go.

He turned it over and said, "When I did my inside mask, it looked a lot like this, dark and angry. I too was surprised to realize how angry I was, considering I was so happy-go-lucky on the outside and everyone seemed to like me and my work."

"Why were you angry?" Claire asked.

Ben hesitated, "It turned out to be post-traumatic stress disorder from a childhood incident."

"Me too," Claire whispered. But she wasn't ready to reveal the ugly side of her either.

"Ok," Ben said.

"Ok," Claire said after a long pause.

Together, they sat there in silence for a while, feeling comforted by the camaraderie.

The pull for liquor and a man had passed.

***

Claire gathered her mask and left. She knew before she called Mercy, that she would have to share this at a meeting and show her mask. Otherwise, this anger was going to kill her. Surprisingly, the anger felt new-founded. But she now understood from the mask exercise, and the artwork "Anger," that it had been simmering for a long time hidden by her sunshiny self, and her need to be loved and protected.

Chapter Forty

The next piece of artwork was huge and heavy, like Claire felt after her mask exercise. Expecting doom and gloom, Claire was surprised to find a colorful garden of sculpted trees within the circular, wood foundation called "Growth and Hope."

Dear Diary... I had fun with this piece. For the foundation, I decided to use a mirror support I had collected from an antique wood vanity table. I love working with a circular base as it represents the world, God and how I am connected.

I used paper mache clay to create a very large tree bending up the right side. I added rusty pieces as the knots of the tree. Rusty reminds me of defects, beautiful yet mysterious. How did a once shiny piece of metal turn rusty and pock-marked?

How does an innocent baby turn into an adult riddled with character defects and the need to eliminate them through alcohol and drugs? Like rusty things, character defects are there for us to examine and let go of when we don't need them anymore.

Again, trees were talking to me. One of the tree branches created a heart. I can't remember if that was on purpose or accidentally on purpose; funny how my higher power works. I filled in the heart shape with a smaller, sculpted, fabric tree.

For the leaves of the larger tree, I used green rice paper secured with gel medium and embellished them with round, pointy seeds the size of golf balls. I had a blast with the embellishments as I also used porcelain art deco flowers that were manufactured for use in lamps around the 1930s and other shiny metal objects.

This piece gave me hope that I can grow and change.

Despite the bright, cheerful colors, Claire couldn't feel hope and growth when she looked at this piece. Trees were a double-edged sword to her. A place to hide, climbing higher into the branches for safety versus the danger and fear on the ground from the switches her father meticulously picked out to whip them with.

The rusty pieces reminded her of how damaged her father was when he was drunk, and how scared, lonely, and sad she was as a result.

She wanted to climb the tree in the piece to get high above the whippings and rage that permeated her home.

She also wanted to sneak a long swallow of vodka. Claire wanted to feel the familiar burning that heated her from her belly outward, erasing her fear.

Instead, she picked up the phone to call Evi, who asked her to say the serenity prayer with her.

"God, grant me the serenity to accept the things I cannot change."

Evi explained that as alcoholics, they could not change the fact that they cannot have one drink—that one is too many and a thousand never enough. That to have one drink will release the dragon all over again, not really addressing the fear, doubt, and insecurities they all felt."

"Fear, doubt, and insecurity," Claire whispered, they continued, "The courage to change the things I can."

Evi explained that, "We ask for courage to not pick up that drink, the courage to focus on something else."

My work, Claire thought, *I can focus on my work.*

They finished with, "And, the wisdom to know the difference."

Evi didn't need to explain the last piece. Claire understood that and was again surprised how a simple prayer could quiet her mind and filled her with a calm that she could only explain as peace and quiet.

Chapter Forty-One

Herb hung "Growth and Hope" and handed Claire the next box. As Herb left, Claire pulled out a canvas painted bright red. It supported a tree pieced together from small pieces of driftwood—construction from deconstruction, wound and bound by stiffened fabric pieces.

> Dear Diary... I am still creating trees as I can feel their spirit and relate to their growth and challenges through storms. I built this tree on a very, very red background. I love red. It is powerful, hot and dangerous. Building this tree was a lot harder and more frustrating than I thought it would be to put a few sticks together. They would not stay still in the glue and kept moving and rolling—like life. Then I got the idea to secure the driftwood with strips of fabric soaked in a gel medium. That was challenging to

weave the fabric in and out of the wood in order to secure them from moving. I suffered blood, sweat and tears but creating this piece pushed me toward growth, through experiencing pain like a tree that bends in the wind or sags from a heavy snow and recovers during the next season to grow more...

Claire hated this piece with a capital "H." Even though she understood the artist's relationship to trees and growth, she only felt her dad's rage and anger as she responded to the intense red background and the sticks. The woven fabric made her feel fragile, like she would fall apart at any minute.

—*As she tried to run from him, she felt the switch and then the blood dripping down the back of her legs. She pushed herself, kept running despite the burning. She, scampered over the fence and almost lost her balance as her dress caught the sharp edges; running right into Aunt Jo's arms*—

She stopped working with this piece and headed for her beloved Madonna and Child.

"Claire, what are you doing out here," June asked concerned. "How is the show going?"

Startled and a little ashamed, Claire was getting ready to lie, but then remembered that only through honesty would she be able to heal and asked, "Can we go to your office?"

Once there, June shut the door and Claire started, "The last couple of pieces I worked on, in addition to the workshop exercises, have sent me into a bit of a tailspin. It seems that I have some healing of my own to do around my own traumatic experiences."

June was empathetic and asked her to go on.

Claire continued with tears in her eyes, "I have to apologize since I didn't tell you everything a couple weeks ago,"

June slid the tissues over.

"I was," Claire gulped for air, "raped and, and, ah beaten," She couldn't stop it now; the whole story came tumbling out in big sobs. "Severely, by a cousin and I lost a baby. I'm learning a lot from this *Art and Healing* collection, but I am also experiencing a lot of memories from my childhood."

Claire couldn't go on with that part of the story. "I feel safer when I am working with the Renaissance Collection, so when the pain gets to be too much to bear, I take a break and spend some time there."

***

June might have been caught off guard if Ben hadn't stopped by to warn her that the collection and exercises may act as a catalyst to expose deep wounds in Claire. She wasn't sure how or what he knew and why she felt he was protecting Claire, but she was glad for the information.

She was quiet as she listed to Claire, got her some water and told her, "Claire, you are safe here. No one is going to hurt you and your job is secure."

Maintaining her professionalism, June continued, "However, I want you to finish curating the *Art and Healing* show, but whenever you need to take a break, please feel free to go back to the Renaissance Collection."

Looking at the clock, June realized that it was late and told Claire she could head out for the day.

***

As Claire walked home, she passed an outdoor café packed with happy hour patrons. She saw business women and men removing their suit jackets; hunky waiters and sexy waitresses served them. The smell of ale and spicy wings hung heavy in the air.

She heard someone call, "Hey Claire come and join us! The party is just getting started."

As she opened the gate to go in, her phone played Rihanna's, "SOS—Someone Rescue Me."

"Step away from the bar," Mercy demanded.

"How did you know?" Claire croaked.

"Because. I can see you."

Claire let go of the gate handle and looked around.

"I'm headed to your place to have dinner with you and Evi. And who do I see, but little miss Claire mesmerized by the sights and sounds of party land across the street."

By the time Claire put her phone back in her purse, Mercy was next to her. She gave Claire a big hug and said, "Let's go."

***

When they got home, Evi was preparing dinner. Claire curled up on the couch with Tabitha and a cup of chamomile tea. Over dinner, she revealed to Evi what happened during the day.

Mercy said, "Welcome to the wonderful world of 'HALT.' We have to be very careful when we get too hungry, angry, lonely or tired. That is when our disease knows we are vulnerable and will provide opportunities to sneak back into our lives.

Claire gave Mercy an evil look and said, "I was doing just fine. I was just checking to make sure that gate handle wasn't loose."

Evi gave her a big hug and said, "Thank you God! Now help me do the dishes."

With that, they all laughed and Claire felt amazed that she healed a bit more that day.

***

Claire was up and ready Saturday morning to go to the gym. It was a lot safer to go early, focus on a real workout, and avoid any temptations with Jose. On her way to workout, she wondered why she hadn't heard from the other Four Amigos. Laughing as she recalled the nickname they gave themselves after they survived their first frat party.

Claire sent a text to Lexie, Adelynn, and Chastity about getting together soon, maybe for Sunday brunch as was once their ritual.

Chapter Forty-Two

Claire carefully removed the next large piece from its thick brown wrapping paper. It was entitled, "Serenity." As the title implied, Claire did get a peaceful sense when meditating on it.

Dear Diary...today I just feel like painting, so I found four medium sized canvases to attack with globs of paint. I love to use a big brush loaded with paint to cover a white background. I love the texture and depth of the paint and the patterns it makes with the brush strokes.

I wanted two blue and two green canvases. I felt like the green had to be thick and permanent; the blue not so substantial. Once finished, I put them together to form a larger piece. I tried to glue and staple them from the back, and that wasn't stable enough. I had some left over canvas that I had painted in a multitude of colors and cut it into strips to secure the four pieces together.

I crisscrossed and glued down the pieces over the front seams to create strength. Funny, but when I hung it up and stepped back it looked like a cross. This was not my intention, since I am not a religious person, but it worked. The physical effort of just painting and the mental challenge to figure out how to unify the pieces into one gave me a very serene feeling that I was coming together; that the pieces of me were starting to fit...

Claire was drawn into this piece; it centered her, calmed her, especially after the emotions evoked from the past week. She liked the painterly brush strokes, and the way the light played off of the paint, thick and dense in places, thin and transparent in others. She liked the feel of the energy where everything came together and how she felt safe.

Similar to how she felt calm and safe around the Madonna and Child. *Impossible*, she thought! How can this abstract painting also make me feel serene like the Madonna and Child? She stopped questioning and allowed herself to feel the peace.

Amazing! Claire thought. During the Renaissance, artists needed skilled technique to properly depict their portraits. Whereas today, this skillful artist, and others like her, used art to express where they are in their lives, working their way through their journey, one creation at a time. *Kinda like a country song telling a story, taking the listener for a ride through the pain and joy of it all.*

***

After work Claire checked for texts from her college friends. Claire called Adelynn to see if she got her text.

Adelynn answered the phone with a cold, "Yes."

At first Claire wasn't sure she had the right number.

"Adelynn," asked Claire, "Is that you?"

"Yes—hi, Claire," snapped Adelynn.

"Did you get my text?"

"Yes, we did."

We? They all got her text and no one replied. *What was going on?*

"So how does this weekend look for Sunday Brunch?"

"It doesn't Claire; we're not available."

"But why not?" Claire heard herself whine.

"Claire, we love you, but we are not available for your failed promises. You have stood us up one too many times and we are not interested in that type of friendship." Adelynn said what needed to be said. No more sitting around waiting for Claire to show up or offer up another lie.

"But what do you mean?" Claire shrieked as she gulped for air.

"My birthday party was the last straw, Claire. Thirty was a big one and you didn't show. In fact, you sounded like you had a horrible hangover and totally forgot. I've got to go."

Claire couldn't get her head around what just happened. *Birthday, when was that?*

She sat down hard on her couch and clicked on the TV. She muted the sound, but the beer in the commercial said in a deep, seductive voice, "*Hey Claire, don't I look good in my gold bottle, all shiny and icy cold? Remember the fun we used to have? I really miss you!*"

Momentarily stunned, Claire said, "Fuck you," loudly to the TV, "You're what got me into this mess in the first place."

She changed the channel, grabbed a bite to eat, and headed to a meeting.

***

For the first time, she really listened and heard someone share her story. She heard what it took to recover. She knew that she had to fix the wreckage of her past if she wanted to get better.

She spoke up to share, "Hi," She started softly, "my name is Claire and I'm an alcoholic." Her apprehension slipped away when she heard the love and acceptance in, "Hi Claire, keep coming back."

She called Mercy when she got home to talk to her about how to fix her life and get her friends back. She also talked about Jeremy and how to end that and be honest about the baby.

***

"First, I know how hard it is to see how unmanageable our lives got while we were drinking. Good for you Claire—you just took your first step. And, it is especially fucked up to know how much we hurt the people we love the most," Mercy said. "The only way we can fix our lives is to be honest, open minded, and willing to forgive ourselves. If your friends are meant to come back and forgive you, they will in their own time. But we have a disease and forgiveness is very important for our own contented sobriety and serenity."

Knowing that Claire would not quite understand, Mercy continued.

"Serenity is the peace and quiet I get, when all that chatter stops between my ears. When all the fear, doubt, and insecurity stops spinning in my head and does not pull me down. It is reaching out to a power greater than yourself, which some call God or higher power."

Mercy knew she had to spill her own secrets, her own experience, strength, and hope to help another drunk recover.

"When I was much younger, I had an abortion. It just about ruined me, as I drank over my loss for years, fucked everything in my path, including girlfriend's fiancés and ruined every relationship in my path. It wasn't until I came into program that I understood how much I hated myself and how what I did hurt other people. I also realized that the abortion was not who I was, but something that happened to me. I was eventually able to forgive myself with God's grace."

After Mercy took a short pause to let Claire absorb everything, she went on,

"Let's do some writing and see what fears, doubts, and insecurities surface and how we can then address them."

"How?" asked Claire.

Mercy explained, "With your higher power, a pen, and a pad of paper, no computer. Find a quiet place to sit, say the serenity prayer, and ask God for guidance to write what you need to see. Let's get back together in a week to talk about it, how's next weekend?"

"Good," said Claire.

Chapter Forty-Three

The next day Claire unpacked a box with three small collages each built around an antique car tail light. They were titled, "Out of the Chaos #1, #2, and #3."

Dear Diary...I am again working on a series of three pieces. I collect corvette tail lights from the late 1960s and early 1970s. They represent stopping to me. I feel a cry rise up as I shout stop the chaos! Stop the addiction! Stop the unmanageable insanity of chasing something, always chasing something to numb the fear, doubt and insecurity that have plagued my entire life. I'm glad I live alone, and only my cats can hear my cries and screams. I'm laughing hysterically as tears streamed down my face staining your pages.

Carefully I glued one tail light in the center of its own canvas. For each piece, I bought three fabrics in the same color family, ranging from dark to light. I then ripped the fabric into one to two inch strips, soaked them in Stiffy, and started to weave them.

As I wove the dark fabrics into the lights, I felt the consequences of my insanity—repeating the same thing over and over yet expecting different results— becoming clearer and yet not getting why it's necessary. I added something in the center of each tail light to represent beauty and sanity as a focus...

Claire liked these pieces. She could feel the chaos of her life untangling as she felt pulled into the center of each one. She was beginning to feel her desperation waning, like she could crawl out of the hole she had created. Things were bubbling up. Claire remembered Mercy's suggestion to write and she pulled out her journal. If anyone walked in it would look like she was taking notes for her show. Pen to paper she started her own diary:

—Before the rape, before losing the baby, my life was manicured and professional during the day—no one knew. By night, I was on the hunt, to quiet the confusion and chaos in my head; to quiet my screaming mind. The only thing that seemed to work was the bottle, and the men who took my body and left my mind in the bar. I thought I was a party girl after all, wasn't I? Was that the truth? Or was it a lie to cover up the real chaos? I realize now that the drinking and men were a lie repeated over and over. They promised me peace and sanity when all they really delivered was out of control

craziness that wouldn't stop. God, if there is hope, please help me.—

Chapter Forty-Four

Claire unwrapped a small, substantial collage entitled, "Through the Storm." It is reminiscent of a turbulent sea. The viewer is forced to look through a black window to a raging, red scene. It is unclear if the artist is looking out at the storm and is now safe or seeing that the storm is still a threat.

Dear Diary...A few days back in the rooms, but I am barely through the storm. Not sure what happened, but at the meeting last night I heard someone say that a break can really be a breakthrough to understand my fear and what triggered that first drink. Right now the only breakthrough I feel is the waves crashing against the rocks in my head.

So I got out a thick six inch by six inch canvas and a square doll house window hoping to find that clarity and calm I see from those in recovery. Instead, I reached for the red and painted a restless center. Then I went to town painting the background a discontented and irritable storm with thick turbulent blue and grey strokes. Instead of a brush I used a palette knife, trying to cut through the confusion and anger...

Claire felt like she was walking through a raging storm. Like the artist, she wanted to push her way through her self-made storm to find the sunshine.

She packed up for the weekend and called Mercy to go over her writing. Mercy was gracious and did not judge what Claire revealed. Claire began to feel safe. She now understood the impact of her drinking on her friends and how she wasn't available for them. How her hangovers sent her into isolation and a desire to be alone to nurse them. How many events had she really missed? Adelynn said that the Thirtieth birthday was the last straw.

Mercy said, "Claire, we don't need to focus on how many times this happened. That is staying in the problem. We don't focus on the problem, we focus on the solution."

"How do I do that?" Claire asked.

"By being honest," Mercy explained.

"But they don't want to talk to me," Claire said, almost in tears.

"I know," Mercy said, telling Claire a similar story from her early recovery. Mercy suggested that Claire write a handwritten note to each of them apologizing for any hurt that she caused them.

"In the note you should tell them about your drinking problem. About how, after college you couldn't stop drinking. That it just got worse and how you lied to them. How you couldn't show up to planned events due to horrible hangovers. Tell them about now and your recovery."

Mercy explained that once Claire sends the letters out that she should let go and let God.

"What the hell does that mean?" snapped Claire. That sounded like the stupidest thing she had ever heard. "What does God have to do with this?" Claire exploded with hot, angry tears racing down her pale face. "He was never there when I needed him as a little girl! My parents wouldn't stop my uncle, prayers to God couldn't stop it, and so I don't believe that God really cares."

Mercy had expected this outburst, remembering her own very clearly. She calmly said, "Claire, I understand that you don't believe that God cares. But God does care, but cannot control what people do. Sadly, there is evil in this world."

Claire did not remember saying that out loud, so how did Mercy know?

Mercy plowed on, "God is a higher power, something greater than us. People in recovery believe in a power greater than themselves to restore them to sanity. We learn to listen to God's will and turn our problems over to him or her so that we don't do evil things.

Some people call it their higher power, some call it God. It might be the God from your childhood and it might be something totally different. Only you can decide. It can be the door knob, the group, or you can borrow my higher power until you find your own. It only has to be a power greater and outside of yourself.

But know this; as long as we keep relying on ourselves, then we stay in the problem, because we keep trying to control it. Just like when I kept trying to control the drink, I ended up drinking more.

The more you push your friends to try to go out and make it the way it was, the more they will push back until there is no chance of any relationship. That is what happened to my first two marriages."

Claire thought she heard herself gasp.

Mercy continued, "It's not until we, and I am going to say it again, let go and let God, that these relationships have a chance to survive and begin to heal.

It helps me to just say a prayer and ask my higher power to bless the outcome. Can you do that?"

Claire, feeling like she was standing in the middle of hell looking back through the window in, "Through the Storm," said she would try.

***

While Claire didn't understand how it worked, she did trust Mercy to guide her in her recovery. So she spent the rest of the weekend in meetings and drafting up the letter that she would send to each of her friends.

Claire even found herself shopping for stationary that was beautiful, thoughtful, and subtly said forgiveness. She was surprised to find that because she was so focused, that she really didn't think about drinking. She printed the letters in her best handwriting, sealed them with a silent kiss, and asked her higher power—whatever that was—to bless these relationships. As she put the letters into the mailbox, she felt the warmth of the sun on her face.

Chapter Forty-Five

B ack at work, Claire continued to review and curate her show and remembered that there were two more pieces in the "6x6" series including the one she held, "Is the Grass Greener?"

Dear Diary...Still feeling unsettled and restless like life is out to get me; I created the second collage in my 6x6 window series. Feeling blah, with little hope, I painted the background black. I actually love the color black and find it to be a very strong color, representing strength. Using black, maybe I will find the courage to not use again.

I used another window frame from a doll house, also painted black. Through the window is a beautiful garden of flowers I found in a magazine. I added two dead wasps from my collection to pollinate them. The flowers represent what I want my life to be. However,

I must beware of the two wasps that could sting me if
I venture into using again...

As she wrote up this piece, Claire felt the darkness closing in
around her. While she could see the flowers through the
window and could almost smell them, she also saw the wasps,
just waiting to sting her.

*—Today was like every day, every time she headed home
from Aunt Jo's; she wished to be invisible, for no one to see
her or to know she was there. But they were like wasps, and
she was like the flower. They could smell her presence and
flew to taste her sweetness. There was no nectar left. They
took that away with their harsh words and belts. They did not
protect her from her uncle, whose hands and mouth had torn
her petals from her stem while stinging her over and over
again—*

Almost dropping "Is the Grass Greener," Claire wondered why
her parents didn't believe her and protect her. How could they
let this happen? And, where was God in all this? How was she
to believe in God and make him her higher power, when he
didn't protect her either?

Claire thought she could control these memories with the liquor, the men, the partying. Not here, not now, not as she got drawn into these paintings.

How can the artist go there and take me with her? Why am I the one who has to curate this show? How can I survive doing it?

She felt sick and was going to take leave. But something told her to hang on and that it would be okay. Maybe that something was her higher power.

Mercy said she had to walk through these feelings to get to the other side so that she wouldn't drink today.

It was almost lunch and she wanted to go sit with the Madonna and Child painting. But as Claire was ready to walk out, her attention was drawn to the "Serenity" painting. She found herself sitting down, staring. She then felt an uncanny presence, like someone sitting next to her, swaddling her in a warm blanket of love, telling her that it was ok. No one could hurt her again. That she did not need to drink anymore.

In a whisper she heard, "I have always been here, I can't control people's will to hurt others like your uncle or parents, but I can provide some solace, like Aunt Jo, when it's possible."

Aunt Jo, she thought as the words caught in her throat. *You showed me the way to Aunt Jo's.* It was more of a statement than a question, knowing that she had found her God, her higher power. That she had just had her spiritual awakening that she had heard and read about over and over again at her meetings, but never understood until now.

She sat there for what seemed like an eternity, relishing her serenity. She now knew that they were just memories and they couldn't hurt her anymore. She was not defined by her uncle's horrid actions or her parents neglect and abuse. Yes, these things had happened to her, but she didn't need to self-destruct over them anymore.

***

On the way home, Claire headed to a meeting and texted Evi and Mercy to meet her.

As soon as they saw Claire they could see it—the serenity—and wondered what happened, or rather, when it happened. They both had their own experience, yet seeing a newcomer, and especially a friend, find it was amazing, reminding them of the power of twelve step recovery programs.

While they were anxious to hear from Claire, they waited until she was ready to share it. When the meeting started, the secretary said that their speaker had to cancel and was there anyone who wanted to lead the meeting.

Slowly, Claire's hand went up and gingerly she walked to stand in front of the room where she told the group of her experience earlier that day. Chills and shivers went through the room as they could feel their own higher powers working in their lives, relieving them of the need to self-destruct over things that they never had any control over; bad people doing bad things.

Chapter Forty-Six

Claire's step felt lighter as she climbed the beautiful marble steps in the NMWA to her gallery to finish writing up the last in the window series called, "The Grass is Greener."

Dear Diary... It was when I woke up, startled, the bed soaked in sweat, that I realized what evil sent me sliding down the rabbit's hole and right into a bar.

It was my brother. But it wasn't a dream; he was at it again with another little girl and I didn't know how to stop it, not directly anyway. The bottle was the only thing that could quiet the unbearable guilt and shame.

I had been sober for about 10 years, thinking I had this thing licked until I saw the physical and mental marks on her. How long had this been going on? The secrets, the lies, and my pain came rushing back. I was about 7 and he was 13, over and over again for years, until I guess I got too old for his tastes. Had he never stopped some 20 years later? Did he just find a new playmate, and this newest one hit way too close to home?

Not until the night of that awful crash did it all finally come to an end. And, so did my last drunk.

They say that we are only as sick as our secrets and that sharing them cuts the sickness in half each time we share. It seemed to work. After the funeral, I walked back into my meetings and told my story.

Other women came up to me to share some of the unmentionable things that happened to them. How they held onto that guilt and despair until it ate away at them forcing them also into the bottle or drugs or both. And, not until they allowed themselves not to own their assailant's actions and move through the full force of the pain to the other side, even if it was like walking through an evil forest in concrete boots through quicksand, did it really stop.

That night, I took their serenity, strength, and courage with me back to the studio and finished the window 6x6 series using bright gold and green paint, mixed for the background. I added more gold to exaggerate more serenity and light. I painted the window black to tie it to the other two pieces and set it against a flower garden topped with a crystal to emphasize clarity. I had finally found some peace and quiet.

Claire was exhausted by the time she finished the third in this series. She could see that the grass was greener and she liked the crystal in the center of the window, but she was worn out and that was it for the day. As Claire worked with Herb to hang up this last piece, her cell phone rang. It was Jeremy.

At first she was excited to hear from him, missing him a little. Then, she remembered what she had to do. Their conversation was brief and they made a date for the next night.

That night, Claire found herself in a bar, or rather on top of the bar, legs spread wide, taking it hard and deep from Mitch. Tommie's hands were kneading her breasts and squeezing her nipples ever so lightly as Jose kissed her mouth deeply. It took everything she had from coming too soon. Too late, she came like fireworks exploding on a clear dark night, lighting up the edges of her mind driving everything else away. Except for Jeremy, who was standing off to the side holding a baby. With the last roll of her orgasm, she woke up by slamming her head into the headboard. The noise was so loud; it woke up Evi who limped as quickly as she could into the room, trying to balance on her crutches.

"What was that? Are you ok?" Evi asked falling next to Claire on the bed.

"I don't know," Claire said, coming out of the fog. Claire sat up confused by the reality of the dream while rubbing the knot popping up on the back of her head. She told Evi about the dream with all of the details.

Evi laughed and said, "I wish I had dreams like that, I never knew you could come in your sleep. Seriously, sometimes when we have using dreams, there is a deeper meaning. Like reminding us how cunning, baffling, and powerful the disease really is."

Claire still startled, replied, "But I wasn't drinking, I was just fucking."

Stifling an even deeper laugh, Evi said, "Yes, but isn't fucking one of the things you used to make yourself feel better?"

"Maybe," Claire said sardonically, "I just like to fuck."

"Right," Evi said, "And, maybe I like limping around on one leg."

With that they both laughed so hard, they almost cried.

"Oh!" Claire said louder than she thought, "I'm seeing Jeremy tomorrow night, an official date to break it off. I know it's time, I am just not sure how much to tell him about the baby."

"Be honest," Evi said, "but not to the point that you hurt him unnecessarily. You have a choice, you can either let him think that he lost a child that might not have been his or you can tell him that it wasn't his and his pain would be about your being unfaithful. What would be the easier pill for him to swallow?"

***

Evi was careful with her words since she knew how easy it is to tell someone what they should do, or what she thinks they should do, but she also knew that she was not supposed to give advice, only suggestions. To recover, Claire would have to own her behavior and determine how to clean up the wreckage of the past.

***

Claire knew now from the dream that she was supposed to relieve Jeremy of the burden of the baby. That symbolically, Jeremy is carrying what he thinks is his baby in his arms; grieving for his baby. She was able to go back to sleep, praying for the courage to know what to say to him.

Chapter Forty-Seven

Work the next day was nice and quiet. Claire took a break from reviewing any new pieces and instead worked with Shelby to review and update any new cards to ensure that they included the *Art and Healing* angle. At the end of the day, she dropped this last stack off at June's office for her final review.

She met Jeremy at their favorite Indian restaurant. She felt sick to her stomach, but ate a little anyway. They engaged in small talk and Jeremy finally said.

"Claire, how are you, really? The last time I saw you, you were in pretty bad shape."

Pretty bad shape, Claire thought. *I'm still in bad shape; you just can't see all the internal bruises.* Instead, she said, "Better. I am getting better and stronger each day."

The meal was over and Claire knew she had to break it off and tell him the truth. She prayed the serenity prayer. Even though she knew that she couldn't control his reaction, she still needed the courage to be as honest as she could.

At that moment, Jeremy took her hand. He began, like the doctor that he was, "Claire, I really love you, but this is not going to work."

She was actually glad that he was doing the breaking up.

"I know," She said as she slipped her engagement ring off her finger. She handed it to him as a tear slid down her cheek.

He started to continue and she interrupted him, "Jeremy, it's okay. I think we are both at the same place with the relationship and it's better for both of us. But, there is one more thing I need to tell you."

Before she lost her gumption, Claire continued, "I'm sorry and don't want to hurt you anymore, but the baby was not yours."

After a long silence Jeremy stood up. He said, shyly, "Thank you for that. I wasn't sure since we haven't really spent that much time together, if you know what I mean. I appreciate your honesty and hope the best for you in the future."

Surprised Claire said, "Me too."

She stood on her tiptoes to give him a kiss on his cheek and one last hug.

As she watched him leave the restaurant, Claire was relieved, yet sad, and asked her higher power to forgive her for any pain she might have caused him.

Chapter Forty-Eight

The next morning, upon reviewing the status of the show, Claire almost yelled out loud and jumped for joy when she realized that there were only two pieces left to curate. She picked the smaller of the two, and carefully removed the brown packing paper to find green eyes staring at her through a blank mask. The title, "Who Am I?" seemed appropriate for this collage.

The mask anchored to the top left corner was enhanced by items from nature. It was balanced in the right lower corner with a rusty item embellished with an apple charm. Claire found this piece disturbing in an odd, appealing way.

Dear Diary...going through my collected stuff, I found a plastic mask that begged the question, Who Am I? I've had this mask for a long time and now is the time to work through that question. Yes, I am an adult child of alcoholics, a victim; scratch that, survivor of incest, and a recovering alcoholic. But there has to be more.

I also discovered some small leather bound poetry books in my stash and tore them up, like I was tearing me apart, looking for the good stuff. I first layered positive verses on the canvas and then haphazardly applied green paint allowing some of the poetry to show through; like the real me is trying to peek out. Then using soft, thick, brown paper soaked in gel medium, I worked really hard to attach that fucking mask.

The process of getting that mask to stay put seemed symbolic for how hard it is to discover who I am under all these layers of junk. I know that I am more than the patterns of my sick family, but I am just not sure how to accept that and move forward.

The mask's probing eyes disturbed Claire. They seemed to say, "Who are you?" Claire, too, wanted to know who she was and how she was going to create new patterns, new dreams for her life. But she was also drawn to the leftover pieces from nature which reminded Claire of long ago memories.

Dead memories always trying to surface, swirling around and around reminding her of a part of herself that she doesn't want to remember, doesn't want to face as part of her. If her parents had only listened to her, and protected her, this dark place wouldn't exist. *Why didn't they protect me? I was only a little girl...*

Claire was surprised how quickly she could be pulled or rather sucked back into devastating memories. Memories that kicked up raw and blistering feelings like she had just removed her hand from a hot stove. Memories she wanted to avoid and would have avoided if she had still been drinking and fucking.

But today she had accepted that neither of those were an option to numbing these feelings. That today, in order to recover, she would have to walk through those memories to get to the other side, even if it felt like she was walking on broken glass in the middle of a firestorm.

From somewhere deep inside, she remembered the following poem:

I cycle in and out of growth
Cycling through old issues and new feelings
Blooming and learning and healing
Feeling and shedding the pain of the past

Marveling in the rawness and beauty of new growth

On her way out of the studio, Claire was surprised to see Ben walking toward her. His lean body and deep blue eyes caused an immediate, overpowering flush between her legs. *Where did that come from?* She wondered, as she worked hard to stay professional.

"Hi," he said, "our Creative Expression workshops are next week and I wanted to check in to see if there is any last minute preparation we need to do."

"Oh, ok, great," Claire bumbled. She knew the art room was on hold for this workshop so she suggested they head upstairs to check on available supplies.

"Where's Cora?" Claire asked, trying to make conversation to distract her from her wet panties.

"She can't join us today, but will be here next week to help with the workshops. Are you excited about your show opening?"

She just about missed the last part of his question as she almost yelled: *Yes! I'm excited, but how did you know? Am I omitting a scent like a cat in heat?*

Trying to answer more subtlety, she said, "Yes, it has been quite a challenge, but I have learned a lot which I hope passes on to the public. Would you like to see it once we are done here?"

"Yes, I would be honored." Ben said, his bright eyes lingering a little too long on Claire's face.

After they checked the art room and confirmed that all the supplies were there, they headed back to the gallery. Claire was heating up as she noticed how Ben looked at her and wanted to take him right there, anxious for the release. She closed and locked the gallery door and turned to Ben, but he was moving away to walk around the exhibit. She waited patiently for what seemed like forever and decided to clean up some of her mess to keep herself busy and distracted from the intense heat rising from her groin.

Ben finally came over to her and said warmly, "Amazing job! You really have captured healing through art! I am so glad we are working together on this project."

In a husky voice, Claire said, "I want to show you one more piece I'm working on."

Taking his hand, she led him into the storage room and like a panther; she pounced on him, pushing him up against the closed door, as she kissed him long and deep. She could feel his excitement mounting as he throbbed hard against her. But Ben pushed her away, maybe a little harder than he intended, saying breathlessly,

"Claire, W—w—wait, we need to stop."

"Why," she shrieked in frustration, "don't you want it?"

"I don't want it," he emphasized, but before he could finish, she was crying hysterically.

The dam had broken, and in between gulps she said, "What's wrong with me? Don't, don't you like me? I could feel that you like me."

Remembering all too well the role sex used to play in his life; he took her into his arms and said gently, "Claire, I like you a lot, actually. I just want to get to know you before we have sex. In fact, I was, am," he corrected himself saying, "going to ask you out this weekend."

"But you don't want me, n—n—now," she gulped out.

"Oh, I want you," Ben tried to conceal a laugh, "I just don't want to confuse sex with love. That doesn't work for me anymore."

"Anymore," Claire repeated in a whisper, "what does that mean?"

"That is a long story for another day," he said. "Can I take you out on a date this weekend? I want to celebrate your show and our new relationship."

"I don't drink," she sulked, tears still sliding down her face. The whole situation seemed useless to her, how could she go out and enjoy herself without a drink. She almost giggled as she thought well, she would have a man.

"Great," Ben exclaimed, "I don't drink either."

Claire was glad that Ben continued to hold her until her tears were spent, feeling that they had just crossed an important bridge.

Claire agreed to Ben picking her up at 6:00pm on Saturday. But she didn't know what this would look like without a drink or a good fuck. This was all new to her, but she really liked Ben and was willing to give it a shot.

Chapter Forty-Nine

On Friday, Claire and Shelby worked on the catalog and hung the last round of cards on the wall next to their pieces. With one piece left to go, Claire was excited, but anxious about the opening.

"Hey," Claire said to Herb, who was preparing the hall and doorway leading into the gallery entrance. The official exhibit banner and write-up would invite and entice visitors into the world of *Art and Healing.*

"Hi Claire don't you worry, everything is coming together nicely for your grand opening!"

"Thanks and have a nice weekend," she said, marveling at how Herb always seemed to know when she needed a little extra assurance.

***

On Saturday, Claire went to an afternoon meeting to get grounded before her date with Ben. She was excited but afraid about how to act and what to talk about, to not ruin it before it got started. She was also embarrassed about the other day in the supply closet.

At the meeting, Claire admitted in her sharing that she didn't know what a real relationship looked like or acted like for that matter. All of her relationships included strong drinks and hard fucking, in no particular order. For that, she got a good round of laughing. When she first attended meetings she didn't understand the laughing. She thought that people were laughing at the person sharing, when all it really meant, was that they understood.

After the laughing stopped, she finished sharing that she didn't have any role models in good strong relationships. Thank goodness other fellows came up to her to share their experience, strength, and hope about how they had learned through program how to be in healthy relationships. They told her to keep coming back and that honesty, open mindedness, and willingness will lead her into the healthy relationships that she deserved.

On her way home, she realized that she did have some good role models—the other Four Amigos. But in the past, she was too busy drinking away her insecurities instead of watching and listening to them.

She turned those thoughts over to her higher power. She knew that once they reached back out to her, that she would suit up and show up to earn their trust back. She would then be available to learn from their relationships with their spouses and children. But she also realized that she would see them in God's time and not hers; helping her to release some of the frustration around fixing those relationships.

***

She and Ben went on their first date and she actually had fun. Dinner was good. They found they had a lot in common with art and their desire to create in one form or another. They seemed to steer away from the deep, underlying stuff that they both needed to heal from, saving that for another day and time. Neither mentioned the incident in the storage closet and for that she was very grateful.

After dinner they went dancing. Ben swirled and twirled her and held her tight during the slow dances. It felt like the prom she couldn't remember attending. However, unexpectantly, the rambunctious scene under the bleaches with her date and some of his football buddies flashed into her head. She told the thought to go away, and thanks for stopping by, but she didn't need it today.

Like a miracle it was gone and so was the obsession to keep playing it over and over in her head and hating herself for trying to be popular with too many blow jobs. By the grace of God, Claire was able to be fully present once again in Ben's arms on the dance floor.

At the end of the night, Ben returned her unscathed to her apartment. He gave her a soft tender kiss and said he would see her next week and asked her out on another date for next weekend.

Glowing, this time in her heart and not between her legs, she said a shy, "Yes, I would like that very much."

***

The next week Claire was busy working beside Ben and Cora doing the Creative Expression Workshops. They had one group of twenty adults and another group of seventeen teenagers that worked their way through the collage, journaling, and mask exercises. At Claire's insistence, Mercy and Evi were part of the adult group.

At the end of the workshop sessions, everyone had a chance to share their experience. Claire was amazed at how much insight the attendees gained and how they, like she, became aware of their issues. As a result, they could accept that they were not at fault, not bad people, and felt confident that they could start to move through some of the stuff that had been holding them back.

Chapter Fifty

On Monday morning, Claire unpacked the last piece. "Out of the Ashes" was an intense piece collaged onto a very large canvas.

Thick painterly flames grew from the bottom up to the middle of the piece. A tree appeared to be reaching out of the flames to grow strong with new leaves. But was it a tree or a woman? There is subtle symbolism throughout which speaks to growth and hope; a wonderful, powerful piece to end the show with.

Dear Diary...I created this piece to depict myself, who like Mother Nature is rising like a phoenix out of ashes. I feel that Mother Nature is very angry for the destruction to the earth; like I am for the destruction to my life. That is why storms seem so violent and unpredictable due to her imbalance; why I feel so violent and unpredictable.

Mother Nature is represented as a tree; I made her face out of an old glass clock encircling a real butterfly that I found and saved for just this occasion. I want desperately to represent time and renewal. I created the leaves of her tree out of the pages of those old small poetry books dyeing them green and layered them on top of the deep blue background.

I made her body out of my old wedding dress. I got a lot of satisfaction from tearing that thing up. Like tearing up a bad memory and making it into something new. Maybe I can tear up my volatility and replace it with patience, tolerance and kindness.

My favorite part was creating the flames. I experimented with a heavy, textured gel medium to create thick paint. I then played with my palette knife to create an inferno of dense red, orange, and yellow flames that popped off the canvas. The flames represent the imbalance and anger around the world's apparent lack of care for abuse, neglect and, as a result, its destruction and possible permanent damage.

Her center is an upside down clock face representing time. Time is valuable because I have time to rise above and through the horrid memories in order to embrace the artist that I am, the healer, and the protector. Today, I am an artist who creates to heal, and heal I will.

Claire felt hot tears rolling down her cheeks as she finished reading the artist's diary. She felt the hope and rebirth from this piece; like she now knew that she too could rise out of the ashes of her past.

That there was a solution and she didn't need to self-destruct anymore over something someone else had done to her. That in order to forgive and heal, she could remember to accept that she hadn't done anything wrong to deserve the abuse.

As she was drying her tears, Herb, walked in. Claire almost forgot that she had called him to help her hang this heavy peace.

Thinking she was distraught, he said, "Claire, don't let anyone steal your sunshine."

He was like an angel in a blue uniform, his wings hidden, yet his actions protecting those around him.

She got up and, giving him a hug, said "Oh, I won't Herb, I promise."

As Herb finished hanging "Out of the Ashes," June stopped by. She wondered around the show, admiring out loud Claire's success.

"Claire congratulations! You have done a wonderful job curating this show."

"Thank you," Claire said looking like a Cheshire cat.

"I trust you will be ready for the opening," June continued.

Deflating like a balloon, Claire said, "Yes ma'am, we will be ready."

Claire saw Herb wink at her, which helped to grow her confidence.

Claire mused at how someone can feel so many things at one time. Because it wasn't an option to numb out today, she accepted her feelings, letting them pass by so she could get back to business.

***

Wednesday night was the opening, so for the next day and a half, Claire, Shelby, and Herb worked hard putting the final touches on the exhibit. Ben and Cora also stopped by to help. June stopped by Wednesday morning for the final stamp of approval and everyone was sent home early to get ready.

Chapter Fifty-One

Claire was excited as she got ready for the show's opening. Normally she would have a drink to steady her nerves, but knowing that wasn't an option, she instead chatted with Mercy and Evi, who were going with her to the opening. As she slipped into her new outfit, she felt whole and beautiful knowing that she had done it. She curated a show by herself and had started to heal.

There was still a lot more healing to do, but she knew that one day at a time, with her higher power, and the fellowship she could do anything.

***

After an early dinner, Claire, Mercy, and Evi took a cab to the opening. Ben, Cora, Shelby, and Herb met them there.

Claire was pleased to see the officials from The Foundation of Art and Healing chatting with June.

The musicians tuned their instruments as the catering staff set up. At exactly 7:00pm, June officially opened the gallery and more people than Claire could count came in. June gave an official welcoming speech and placed Claire beside her to greet their visitors and supporters.

About an hour and a half later when the line finally died down and everyone settled in to enjoy the show, June came up to Claire and said there was someone she wanted Claire to meet—the artist. Claire didn't realize that they knew who the artist was.

As Claire turned around, there stood a tallish, middle-aged woman. She was slim with short, spiky, grey hair and black owl glasses that emphasized her sparkling green eyes. She was dressed in a black bohemian top which housed a multitude of colorful butterflies; it flowed over black jeans that were tucked into purple cowboy boots.

Claire's heart caught in her throat and everything became very clear as she felt those familiar arms come around her. It was Aunt Jo.

CPSIA information can be obtained at www.ICGtesting.com
Printed in the USA
BVOW01s0457150914

366574BV00002B/7/P

9 781632 634245